Howard Gurney was born in S
author of six novels and mul
journal articles. He works as a medical oncologist at Westmead Hospital in Sydney and is also a professor of medicine at Macquarie University, where he undertakes clinical trials for cancer patients. His first fantasy fiction novel, *Twin*, was published in 2015.

He lives in Sydney with his wife and their five children. He has also worked in Manchester, UK and travels extensively.

Other books by Howard Gurney

Path to Chaos series (fantasy)
*Twin*
*The Thread Frays*
*Chaos*

Dr Christopher Walker Murder Mystery series
*Murder on the Ward*
*Death in a Chapel*
*Murder at The Rocks*

# MURDER ON THE WARD

## A Dr Christopher Walker Murder Mystery
## Book 1

Howard Gurney

*This is a work of fiction and the characters are imaginary*

Copyright © Howard Gurney 2020

All rights reserved. No part of this book may be reproduced or transmitted in any form or by any means, electronic or mechanical, including photocopying, recording or by any information storage and retrieval system, without the prior permission in writing from the publisher.

ISBN 978-0-6487177-0-6

Print edition 2020

# CHAPTER ONE

CHRISTOPHER WALKER HELD his breath under the water as he was buffeted by the frenzied currents. He flailed around, searching.

She had to be near!

Her hand had slipped from his only a moment ago. It was dark and his lungs were bursting. He'd have to push himself to the surface soon to catch a breath or he'd drown. But if he did, he'd lose her.

He was hot despite the water but his leg felt cold. He kicked out but something had wrapped around it, stifling him. What if he couldn't get to the surface? Any moment he'd be forced to take a breath and his lungs would fill with water.

He groaned and kicked again.

He had to breathe! He sucked in deeply, knowing it would be his last.

Walker woke up in darkness, gasping air into his lungs as if he had just run a race. The bedsheets were wrapped around his legs, trussing him like a victim, and he fought to escape. Finally he was free and he sat on the edge of the bed, panting.

A summer storm pelted on the windows of his bedroom and he could hear water rushing in the gutters of the street below. Despite the rain, it was stifling. The mosquito coil on his bedside table had burned out but the tangy odour hung in the hot air.

An orange light flickered through the window onto the ceiling. He lurched towards the balcony doors and, gasping for air, flung them open, only to be immediately assaulted by a blasting easterly gale. The branches of a tree whipped above him and within a moment he was drenched. He stepped out and stood hunched at the veranda rail, welcoming the chill wind that lashed his body, feeling the needles of rain drumming into his face. He breathed the cool air deeply and looked down onto the street below. There, a garbage truck went about its solitary chore, heedless of the storm. He watched as the robotic arms reached past a car to pick up a green wheelie bin and deposit the contents into the metal maw of the truck.

The bin thumped back down onto the kerb just as an arc of lightning flashed across the southern sky over the hill above, immediately followed by a mighty crack of thunder that left his ears ringing and the air sizzling. He jerked away from the metal rail in fear. One of his friends had been killed by lightning on a school excursion years before.

The garbage truck turned the corner and all noise faded, leaving only the howl of the wind and the drum of the rain on the tin roof of the veranda. He stood in the doorway watching the raindrops dance on the bitumen in the small circle of light cast from the streetlamp opposite.

Why did she let go? He had always thought her hand had slipped, but in his dream he had the distinct impression that she had pushed away from him.

Then that awful, familiar feeling came over him, of a hole forming in his chest that threatened to suck his heart into it, taking his breath away. He forced himself to keep breathing as he stumbled back inside, leaving the balcony door swinging in the wind, and collapsed into an armchair, his guts heaving. He clutched the arms hard, feeling the rough fabric of the upholstery against his skin.

It was the only thing of hers left.

Flea was gone.

Everything was gone.

He was empty.

There was nothing left.

Just the Black.

## CHAPTER TWO

THE FIGURE ENTERED the hospital room and closed the door quietly – blue hospital gown, paper mask, hair cap and latex gloves.

In the bed lay an elderly Asian man, propped up on a pillow reading a newspaper. He frowned at the intrusion.

'Sorry to disturb you, professor. I need to pop a cannula in for your treatment.' The voice was muffled by the mask.

The patient grimaced but said nothing as he put down the paper and held out his arm. Deft fingers swabbed the skin and inserted the small plastic tube into a blood vessel below the skin surface, tethering it quickly with tape.

'Now just a little injection. Please relax.'

The professor looked down at his arm as the contents of a syringe were slowly pumped into his vein. The figure pulled down the mask. For a moment, the professor's eyes widened, then his body relaxed, all movement ceasing except for the subtle respiratory flow of his chest.

'There you are. I know you can still hear me. I know you can still breathe – just.' Curious eyes stared eagerly at the patient's slack face, the pupils just visible between the slit of his eyelids.

'Now I want you to hear my story. It's a very sad story. But don't worry, I'll be fast.'

The murderer paused, as if savouring the moment.

'I want to make sure you hear all of it.'

Lips curled into a smile.

'Before you die.'

# CHAPTER THREE

'IT'S AMAZING WHAT you become used to,' said Dr Christopher Walker.

He placed a comforting hand on the shoulder of the young woman who sat hunched over before him on a bed on the fifth floor of Western Meadows Hospital in the western suburbs of Sydney.

Hairless and gaunt, she heaved up yet another gutful into the green plastic bowl on her lap, to the extreme discomfort of the circle of medical students gathered around.

'In my younger days,' Walker smiled towards the students, 'this would have been enough to have me hurling.' He patted the woman's shoulder. 'Now it doesn't bother me at all. Belinda here could vomit right onto my shoes and I wouldn't even turn a hair.'

He raised his eyes expectantly at the students. The closest one, a large fellow with the shoulders of a front-row forward and face the colour of a Paspaley pearl, fought to stifle a retch, his mouth hanging open like a sick dog. Another – a thin girl in a short white coat that matched the pallor of her face – clasped her hands tightly against her abdomen before turning on her heels to flee the room, two other students following closely in her wake.

Walker turned back to his patient, his face softening. 'Now, Belinda, don't worry. You'll be feeling much better by tomorrow, I promise. In the meantime, we'll give you something to help.'

He turned to a nurse who hovered nearby, patting the patient's hand. 'Jennifer, I'll write up some dexamethasone and metoclopramide and we'll increase the drip rate. When Belinda's a bit better we'll give her two milligrams of lorazepam so she can sleep it off.'

'Sure, Chris.'

Elfin in her tight blue uniform with blonde hair tied back from her pretty face, she could have been a schoolgirl. But she moved towards the door with swift efficiency and called back over her shoulder with the voice of a mature woman. 'I'll get the chart.'

'This is why we need better anti-emetics,' said Walker, addressing the students who remained. 'We'll cure Belinda's germ cell tumour but this cisplatin chemotherapy is torture for some.' He frowned down at Belinda, who wiped her mouth with a towel as some of the colour returned to her face. 'Ondansetron has been approved but we need to get it on the formulary quick smart so we can use it. If we get the hospital to pay for it, that is. This is 1991, after all.'

The nurse returned with two syringes on a tray and proceeded to fiddle with the plastic clamp that controlled the rate of the intravenous drip in the patient's arm.

Walker moved towards the door and waved his students after him. 'That will be enough for today's tute. Let's meet same time next week. In the meantime, do some reading around anti-emetics – types and mechanism of action, that sort of thing.'

The students trailed away and he stopped at the sink to wash his hands. On the wall above was a mirror and he glanced at it as he soaped up his hands. Reflected back was a thin face that matched his thirty-two years – a long furrowed forehead and sandy-coloured hair. He forced his eyes back to his hands; he hated looking at himself. If he lingered too long, the Black might come. It was always there, just below, ready to rise and take him. Judge him.

He wiped his hands dry and glanced at his wristwatch then raised his eyes to the entrance of the ward to see a beautiful Asian woman striding through the double doors, dressed in a long white coat.

'Right on time as usual,' he said under his breath.

His eyes flicked over her while she moved towards him as he leaned on the nurses' station, trying not to stare. She was tall and thin with long lustrous hair pulled back from her face to display smooth olive skin, high cheekbones and a long straight nose. She was dressed impeccably beneath her white coat in a skirt and buttoned top, and expensive-looking heels. Even from here he could see she was wearing the pearl earrings and gold and jade necklace he'd noticed on her a few days before.

'Your new registrar's pretty, isn't she?' said a voice at his shoulder, causing him to start. Jennifer the nurse stood beside him, holding the empty syringes.

Walker shifted uneasily and looked down at the notes. 'Hadn't noticed.'

Jenny looked at him out of the corner of her eye and smiled. 'Nice body too. It's not fair – those Asian girls have got such nice firm backsides.'

Walker glanced down over Jenny's shoulder. 'Really, Jenny? Yours is not bad at all. I wouldn't be too jealous if I were you.'

Jenny fluttered her eyes in an exaggerated fashion. 'Dr Walker,' she gasped in mock astonishment. 'I'm a married woman. I'll have you keep those sorts of comments to yourself or I'll register a complaint.'

He rolled his eyes. 'Does your husband approve of you showing off your body to all and sundry in that uniform?'

Jenny smirked innocently. 'I don't know what you mean.'

'Dr Walker,' interrupted the young doctor, nodding a welcome as she reached them. 'Hi, Jenny.' She had the cultured British accent of a highly-educated Singaporean.

'Hi, Angela,' said Jenny. She dipped her head towards the nearest room. 'Belinda's been sick. We've just given her something for it.'

'Poor thing,' she said with genuine concern. 'That cisplatin chemo's nasty stuff.'

'Don't tell me, tell him,' said Jenny, jabbing her thumb at Walker. 'He's the one who ordered it.'

Walker took an exasperated breath but before he could answer, Angela raised an admonishing finger at Jenny. 'You have to be cruel to be kind,' she said smoothly.

He smiled. 'Couldn't have said it better myself.'

'I thought you lot took an oath to "first do no harm",' Jenny bantered good-naturedly.

'Belinda won't thank us if we don't cure her,' said Angela.

'Yes, the worst thing you can do to your patient is underdose them,' said Walker. 'Or even worse, give them a useless treatment just to avoid making them sick. Only a gutless oncologist would do that.'

Jenny raised her hands as she walked back towards Belinda's room. 'Well, I've said my piece. I'll let you two get on with your round.'

'Do you think she means it?' said Angela as they watched her go.

'No,' said Walker. 'Well, maybe a bit. The ward nurses hardly ever see the cured patients six months later. They only see them sick as a dog and throwing up in a hospital bed. Or worse.'

'Dead,' added Angela.

He grunted. 'Let's get on with the round.' He stared around at the knot of young doctors and nurses gathered at the central nurses' station. 'Where's our intern? What's his name again?'

'*Her* name. Gloria. She's in Casualty doing an admission. Shall I page her?'

'No, leave it, we'll be faster without her.'

Angela frowned. 'She'll never learn if you keep doing that. You're already in trouble with the clinical super. As a consultant medical oncologist in a teaching hospital, you're supposed to actually teach, you know. You are the expert in germ cell cancers, after all. This will be her only chance to learn anything about them.'

Walker groaned. 'I know. But I hate teaching interns. I'll tell you what, I'll teach you and then you teach her. How's that?'

'You're happy enough teaching medical students,' said Angela, stepping in beside Walker as he moved away.

'That's different.'

'How so?'

'I don't know, it just is.' He looked up at the board listing the names and bed numbers of the patients on the ward. 'Who's first?' Then he gave a short grunt. 'Hey, look, Professor Benjamin Chee is an inpatient. I wonder what for?'

'Radioactive iodine therapy,' said Angela. 'Thyrotoxicosis.'

'Really? Poor bloke. An overactive thyroid? You wouldn't have guessed it with his boring personality.' He dropped his voice. 'He's a total dickhead. No one can stand him. Still, I wouldn't wish that upon anyone.'

'Really? Is that what everyone thinks of him?'

'Yeah. Great rheumatologist but a total prick. Personality disorder for sure. Sociopath.' Walker turned to her, surprised. 'Haven't you ever come across him?'

'Of course,' she said matter-of-factly. 'He's my father.'

Walker spun fully to face her. 'What? Why ... why didn't you tell me?' he spluttered. 'I'm sorry for saying that about your father. Totally uncalled for.' He looked around, flustered, trying to determine whether anyone else had overheard. 'Why didn't someone tell me?'

'It's okay. I agree with you. Maybe I wouldn't have used those words, but the sentiment's the same.'

Walker looked at his registrar closely. She didn't seem upset but maybe she was hiding it. The flawless skin of her forehead remained smooth. He dropped his voice. 'Listen, Angela, I can do the round myself if you want to go and be with your father.'

Now she *did* frown, looking genuinely surprised. 'Why would I want to do that? My father doesn't need me.'

'Are you sure?' Walker insisted. 'Perhaps we should stick our heads in to make sure. I should say hello to him myself. He is one of my fellow physicians, after all.'

'If you insist. You're the boss.'

They made their way to Room 63, lead-lined and used for radioactive iodine therapy. Walker peered through the narrow glass panel. 'Looks like he's asleep.' He turned to Angela, who stood close behind him, squinting over his shoulder.

'We shouldn't disturb him then,' she said.

He turned back to the professor. 'I'll just poke my head in.' He cracked the door and stepped into the room but kept hold of the door. 'Benjamin, it's Chris Walker here. And I have Angela with me. Your daughter.'

There was no movement from the mound on the bed.

'Professor?' said Walker. When there was no reply, he raised his voice. 'Sorry to disturb you.'

'Father,' Angela said. Walker noted the lack of affection in her voice.

Professor Chee still failed to reply.

'Let's leave him,' said Angela.

Walker considered doing as Angela said but there was something about the way the professor was lying – the lack of movement. He opened the door and walked into the room. But Angela pushed past him, went to the bed and placed her fingers over the carotid artery in his neck. 'He's dead,' she said quickly, her voice flat.

'Dead? Are you sure?' But one look at his pale face and cyanotic lips told Walker the truth. 'I'll call an arrest.' He pressed the call button three times then shoved Angela aside and threw the blankets off the body. Kneeling up onto the bed, he proceeded to compress the chest as Jenny ran into the room.

'I'll call a resus,' she yelled and ran out again.

'Give him mouth-to-mouth, Angela,' Walker shouted. But oddly, the girl stepped away, her face blank, and stood at the edge of the room, looking on with a strange detachment.

'I told you. He's dead.'

Moments later the room was full of people. The cardiology team charged in with the arrest trolley. The registrar slapped moistened paddles onto the professor's chest. The anaesthetic registrar had him intubated quickly and began ventilation with a black airbag. Another doctor dug a cannula into a vein in the neck and set up a drip. As Walker stepped away, he noticed Chee already had a small blue-banded cannula in his left forearm.

All eyes went to the monitor, which showed a flat line with the occasional blip of an electrical impulse.

'Bradycardia,' called the cardiology registrar. 'Is there a pressure?'

The nurse shook her head. The anaesthetic registrar stopped pumping the bag and felt for a pulse in the neck. 'Nothing,' he said, then continued the ventilation.

'Adrenalin,' called the cardiology registrar. The cardiology nurse had already drawn it up and she injected it into the plastic bung of the fast-running drip. They stared hopefully at the monitor but there was no change.

'Again,' said the cardiology registrar and the nurse pumped another ampoule of adrenalin into the drip. After a moment's examination of the trace, he shook his head. 'Still nothing. Give me a spinal needle. And run in some bicarb.'

The cardiology registrar grabbed an adrenalin-filled syringe from the nurse and felt for the bottom of the sternum and pushed the needle in, aiming towards the left shoulder, then sucked back dark blood to confirm he was in the heart. He injected the drug then looked up at the monitor. 'Not working. Give me another.'

The fourth ampoule of adrenalin was injected but Walker noticed the ECG trace was now a flat line. He had led a large number of resuscitations himself when he was a training physician and he knew Angela's father would not survive. She remained in the corner of the room looking on, her face expressionless. He had to get her out.

'Come, Angela, we should leave.' He placed a firm arm around her shoulder and moved her gently towards the door. She merely nodded and let him escort her outside into the corridor.

'They're wasting their time,' she said, her voice cold. 'He was already dead when we went in.'

Walker held her hand softly. 'I'm sorry, Angela. No one should see their father go like that.'

She raised her head stiffly. 'No one has a father like mine.' Her brown eyes held his, hard and emotionless. 'I can assure you, he will not be missed.'

# CHAPTER FOUR

FORTY MINUTES LATER the unsuccessful resuscitation team left, trudging along the corridor towards the coronary care unit, talking among themselves, their minds already on other tasks. Jenny had taken Angela away for a cup of tea and Walker lingered in the corridor outside Room 63. He had a feeling there was something odd about the whole affair but he just couldn't put his finger on it. He'd been to many resuscitations and the one he'd just witnessed unfortunately ended like most of the others. But there was something he'd seen ... or maybe heard.

Something didn't add up. He could feel it in his bones, and he'd learned over the years of being a clinician to pay attention to that feeling. On many occasions it had led to him diagnosing conditions that had stumped others, or had encouraged him to select certain treatments, ultimately to the patient's benefit, when the initial evidence pointed elsewhere. He didn't believe in strange senses, just that his intuition was a meld of many years of forced study as well as experience garnered from the countless patients he'd treated, all stuffed inside, layer upon layer, which somehow his subconscious could tap into.

He opened the door and looked at the aftermath of the resuscitation. Walker had already reviewed Professor Chee's file. He'd been admitted for routine radioactive iodine for an overactive thyroid that almost certainly would have been fixed by the therapy. He had no cardiac history, and by all reports was otherwise well. Since there was no obvious cause of death, it would be referred to the coroner. Consequently, the body lay on the bed with all the tubes still in place, ready for the autopsy.

Walker moved to the side of the bed and lifted the sheet. The pyjama top had been hastily pulled closed but remained unbuttoned and he could see the clear gel hat had been smeared over the chest for the resuscitation paddles. Chee's dead eyes peeked out at him from beneath not-quite closed lids and he hesitated. He pushed down gently on the cold eyelids but they wouldn't close, cracking open again when he released the pressure.

'What am I doing here?' Walker murmured to himself. Someone was sure to come in and wonder why he was lingering in the room with a dead body. Since the death was a coroner's case, his actions would look suspicious. 'Intuition!' he huffed.

He started to step away, then paused when his eye caught the small blue cannula in the left forearm. Why did the professor have a cannula? He was pretty sure it wasn't the protocol for radioactive iodine therapy, which was given orally. And it was 25 gauge, a small one generally used only for difficult veins or a once-off infusion. The tethering was untidy, with a single piece of white tape rather than Steri-Strips crossed over to ensure the cannula would not dislodge.

Walker lifted the arm to examine the cannula more closely when he noticed a glint of light from the sheets next to the body. The sun was shining in through the west-facing window and had caught something. He leaned over, squinting – it was the top of a glass ampoule that had been discarded after opening. He was about to dismiss it when he realised it was on the wrong side of the body, all the resuscitation activity having taken place on the other side. He picked it up and held it carefully between his fingertips to closely examine it. The glass stub was clear with a yellow ring around the base at the line where the crack in the ampoule would have been made. He didn't immediately recognise it, but it had been years since he'd personally given an injection.

The door swung open and a lanky wardsman arrived, followed by two nurses ready to take the body to the morgue. Walker knew the wardsman by name, and Andy Korbmann hesitated when he saw him, his eyes dropping to the glass stub in his fingers. Walker stepped away quickly and slipped the stub into his pocket, then motioned for them to proceed, taking up a place at the edge of the room. A nurse unhooked the IV bag and placed it on the body while the others fussed around with the bed linen, then the three of them expertly lifted the body and placed it carefully into a long wheeled tub that was disguised as a trolley. Korbmann fitted a tight blue plastic cover over it to make it look like an empty trolley, so as not to upset the patients when they moved through the ward.

Soon they were gone and Walker surveyed the empty room. The sheets were a tangled knot at the foot of the bed and the floor on the right side was littered with torn plastic packaging and cardboard boxes of drugs, looking much like the aftermath of any other resuscitation he'd seen. But he still couldn't help feeling that something was amiss.

He shrugged and decided to get on with his round. He looked up and down the corridor, which was now bustling with staff getting back to their normal chores. 'Now where is that bloody intern?'

Jenny was walking towards him when he came out. 'How's Angela?' he asked.

The petite nurse frowned. 'She seems to be fine. Strangely so. She was ... distant, but I wouldn't say upset. She said she wanted to go back to work but I insisted she go home.'

'Of course. Strange reaction though. When she said he was dead, it was like a statement of fact. She didn't seem concerned. She and her father obviously didn't get on.'

They walked together back to the nurses' station.

'What about his wife?' he asked.

Jenny shook her head. 'There isn't one. Angela's mother died five or six years ago.'

'Her mother died? Any other family?'

'She says she's an only child.'

Walker looked thoughtful, then hesitant. 'Does she have anyone?'

Jenny raised an eyebrow. 'Is that curiosity or care?'

'Care, of course.'

'Don't know,' she answered. 'Where are you going?' she added as Walker moved away.

'To find the clinical super. Someone needs to keep an eye out for her.'

# CHAPTER FIVE

WALKER PULLED UP his old silver BMW convertible before a two-storey terrace in Lower Fort Street, Millers Point, breathed out deeply and switched off the engine. It had been a long, hot drive home in traffic and he needed a beer. The air was heavy with the perfumed scent of jacaranda, the trees obviously having recovered after the hailstorm that had swept Sydney two weeks before. Now that he wasn't moving, the humidity pushed down on him from the surrounding terraces like a sauna. He'd driven home with the top down but halfway along Victoria Road, moving through Gladesville and Drummoyne at not much more than walking pace, he'd regretted his decision, the fumes and grit abolishing the carefree feeling he thought the open top would provide.

The car radio blared 'The Horses' by Daryl Braithwaite, and although the ex-lead singer of Sherbet wasn't normally one of his favourites, the freedom of the ballad had relaxed him as he'd snaked the last kilometre home, so he sat and listened until the song finished. The beeps for the seven o'clock news overlaid the last few notes and Walker paused to catch the headlines.

*It has been claimed today that the three US soldiers who died in the Battle of Khafji in late January, as part of Operation Desert Storm, were killed by friendly fire* – He turned off the radio. He was in no mood to listen to the craziness of the Gulf War.

Sweat coated his back and underarms and he glanced at the dark windows of his terrace, contemplating whether he should have a shower before going to the pub. But then he caught the sound of an acoustic guitar and a jagged voice wafting up the road and saw through his rear-vision mirror the beckoning doors of the Hero of Waterloo behind him. He made up his mind. Salivating at the promised taste of a pilsener, he jumped out of the car and quickly unfolded the top, clicking it back into place.

James worked behind the bar. A long string bean of a man with a foppish mop of hair and a prominent Adam's apple, Walker always had to check himself from calling him Jim. He felt the laconic barman was definitely a 'Jim' and couldn't understand why he got so shirty when anyone named him so.

By all appearances, James hadn't even seen him enter but as Walker reached the bar, a schooner of amber ale was set before him, topped by a satisfying head. Walker licked his lips and downed half of it before looking around the small bar. The Hero was one of Sydney's oldest pubs and, like most of the original colonial buildings, was crafted from local sandstone. A timber bar ran the length of the narrow room and on the far wall hung a portrait of the hero himself – Arthur Wellesley, the Duke of Wellington. It was a Thursday night and the bar was comfortably full with office workers and uni students leaning close to each other, shouting to be heard, getting a head start on the weekend.

On the dais, a skinny dude dressed all in black was belting out a Meatloaf tune, smashing violently on his Maton Dreadnought, fighting to be heard over the hubbub.

A chubby girl with dyed blonde hair, dressed in a too-short leather skirt, gyrated in the space before him, clutching a wineglass in one hand and thrusting the other fist into the air in time with the music.

Walker nodded to James and made his way to a small table close to the front door where a middle-aged woman with silver hair sat sipping on a middy of beer and smoking.

'How's things, Shirley?'

She grimaced. 'Could be better, Chris. Hawke wants to stick his nose into the wharfies' affairs. A lot of our members are nervous.'

There was news that Prime Minister Bob Hawke was negotiating to end the stalemate in a waterside dispute that was threatening to cripple the harbour. Walker knew all about it. His father, now dead, had worked on the wharves at Millers Point and Walsh Bay all his life. Walker wasn't a fan of the Waterside Workers' Federation. He thought they were greedy and corrupt but he knew he wouldn't get anyone around here to agree with him. He'd lived with his father in Lower Fort Street all his life, so was no stranger to the unions and what they got up to. His mother had died when he was five and his father had gone the same way from lung cancer seven years ago, when Walker had just started his specialist training. At least no one had tried to give his father chemotherapy. Walker knew now, more than anyone, how useless it would have been for his father's type of lung cancer.

He grunted noncommittally at Shirley, wanting to change the subject. 'Hot as hell out there, isn't it?' He took another gulp of his beer.

She pointed at him with her cigarette, held between two fingers. 'Chris, I know you don't like the unions but if it wasn't for them, we'd have no home.' She jabbed a thumb towards the front door. 'There'd be no Rocks. All of this'd be gone and you along with it. If it wasn't for Nita and Jack Mundey back in the seventies, you'd be living out at Bidwell. We owe them our support.'

In the early 1970s, the local residents' action group combined forces with the NSW Builders Labourers Federation under the leadership of Jack Mundey, to set up green bans that saved much of Sydney's heritage, including the historic nineteenth-century buildings and housing commission terraces in The Rocks from being demolished to make way for office towers.

Walker raised his hands. 'I know, Shirley. It's just not my thing anymore. I've got cancer patients to look after.'

She had the thick voice of a lifelong smoker. 'We've all got someone to look after, Chris. But there are bigger things than a few sick people who you probably can't do anything for anyway.' She pointed outside the pub door. 'This is our community. If we don't save it, no one will. Our families have lived here longer than any others. We can both trace our ancestors back to the first colony.' She jabbed her finger into his shoulder. 'We owe them.'

Walker bowed his head. 'Okay, Shirley. I promise I'll help.'

'Come to the RAG meeting next Tuesday night then. It'll be the first for the year. You have to show your support.'

The Rocks Resident Action Group met in the Garrison Church across the road from the Hero of Waterloo on the second Tuesday of every month.

Walker downed the rest of his pilsener. 'Don't worry, Shirley, I'll be there.'

On the short walk home, Walker breathed in the heady scent of the jasmine and paused to look up and down the street. At one end, he could see the Garrison Church, or Holy Trinity as it was properly called, the yellow sandstone walls shining in the bright spotlights. Down the street in the opposite direction, the massive arch of the Harbour Bridge rose up, obliterating the view of the water, and he wondered what it would have looked like in his ancestors' time. His great-great-grandmother had arrived in 1790 on the Second Fleet, banished as a convict for theft, sent from London to the other end of the earth, never to return. She married a sailor, Christopher Walker, and the family had lived in The Rocks ever since, mostly existing as dockside workers. A great-uncle of his had contracted the bubonic plague in 1900 and the disease had then spread through the dockworkers at Millers Point. That was one of the things that had spurred his interest in medicine. That and not wanting to be poor all his life like his father.

One of the local cops had caught him stealing and scared the living daylights out of him, made him rethink his future. After that, he'd done well at school, much better than anyone expected, and before he knew it, he'd got into medicine. His father initially didn't believe it – thought he was pulling his leg. But then he was ecstatic, shouting drinks at the Hero for all the locals to celebrate.

For the first year of uni, Walker thought they had made an error with his marks so he'd got into medicine by mistake. Most of the other students were from private schools and he thought they were much smarter than him. He'd worked his guts out, studying hard so he wouldn't be unmasked as a fool. But then the exam results came rolling in – distinctions and high distinctions mostly. It wasn't until the third year of medicine that Walker finally believed that he was as good as everyone else. Before he knew it he'd graduated with honours and got a placement into one of the best teaching hospitals in Sydney.

A few years later, the same year Walker was accepted into the specialist physician training scheme, his father was diagnosed with lung cancer. After his father died, it was a natural progression for him to specialise in medical oncology. Felicity had been with him all the way, supporting him, from his first year of medicine to the year he had taken off training to go to New Guinea.

And then she died.

He paused in the act of pulling his keys from his pocket as the memories – horrible ones – flashed through his mind. He squeezed the keys tight, the metal biting into the palm of his hand as the Black threatened to grab him. He didn't want to think of it.

His secret.

He shook his head and clamped his jaws together, forcing himself to think of something else, anything to keep the Black away. He let out a shaky breath. Something else like the death of Professor Chee. Slowly, slowly, his mind calmed as he focused on the circumstances surrounding the death of his colleague.

'Yes, something is not quite right there,' he said to himself as he turned the key to his front door.

# CHAPTER SIX

THE MEDICAL ONCOLOGY clinics of Western Meadows were held in the bowels of the hospital in the Radiation Oncology Department, which had been founded in the late 1970s by a boisterous Scotsman by the name of Hew McGregor, a towering man both in stature and personality.

Medical oncology was a relatively young discipline and only came to the Western in the mid 1980s and was still seen as the younger cousin by the more established radiotherapy fraternity. A few of the radiation oncologists still gave chemotherapy for breast cancer, rather than the medical oncologists, and since they were quite good at it, no one complained. The med oncs were busy enough.

Walker finished with his last patient for the morning, an elderly fellow with small cell lung cancer whose tumour had returned after an initial response to the first line of chemotherapy treatment. The carboplatin and etoposide had worked well, keeping the cancer away for more than a year, but now it was back in his liver and adrenals, and Walker had spent a long and difficult conversation with the man and his eldest daughter about whether they should try more treatment. The follow-up treatment was less effective and more toxic. It made the hair fall out and caused vomiting, and some oncologists didn't recommend it. However, the daughter had insisted and eventually both Walker and the patient had acquiesced.

Angela had seen the patient first and had then sat in on the consultation. 'What do you usually give?' she said after the patient and his daughter had left.

'OCA,' said Walker. 'Vincristine, cyclophosphamide and doxorubicin.'

She frowned. 'That acronym doesn't work.'

'Brand names,' said Walker. 'Look it up.' He thought she should know about the common treatment regimen, but then he remembered she was less than a week into her advanced training. 'Oncovin is the brand name for vincristine. The same goes for Adriamycin and doxorubicin.'

Angela nodded. 'Okay, I'll phone chemo and book it in.'

Walker chatted with the nurses while he waited for his registrar. Today he was wearing a bright red tie and the nurses joked about how it matched the garish colour scheme of the department. The hospital was built in the late 1970s and had adopted the trendy colours of the time – bright green and burnt orange – a theme that was repeated in the furniture, handrails and protective wall panels throughout the wards and clinic areas, but now considered terribly outdated and in poor taste.

'Your dressed nicely today, Chris,' said one of the nurses, smiling. 'Trying to impress your new registrar?'

The other nurses giggled and raised their eyebrows suggestively.

Walker raised his own eyebrow in mock frustration. It was widely known that he wasn't married or, as far as the nurses could tell, even had a steady partner, so they were ruthless in their pseudo-matchmaking. He wondered what they said when he wasn't around. The Rad Onc nurses were renowned for creating all sorts of scurrilous gossip, especially of a sexual nature. He knew it helped them cope with the difficult job of dealing with cancer patients every day.

He studied Angela as she spoke on the phone. She certainly was attractive and, as far as he could tell, not much younger than him. She wore a tight floral skirt that came to her mid-thigh, showing long shapely legs and smooth olive skin. Still, there was something about her that was unsettling. Her father had died the day before but, by all appearances, she was going about her day as usual. He was surprised she had even come to work. He understood everyone coped with grief differently, some throwing themselves into their work to forget. But Angela gave the impression that she didn't care; worse, she seemed even uplifted by the loss of her father.

She finished on the phone and turned to him.

'All done?' he said. 'Shall we go?'

They walked out of the dimly lit department through automatic doors into a bright sunlit courtyard where the humid summer heat hit them. A few nurses sat under a shady gazebo, smoking and laughing with one of the wardsmen, and the late January sun beat down on the pavers making Walker break out into a sweat. He glanced at Angela who seemed unaffected by the heat.

She seemed to know what he was thinking. 'I love this weather,' she said, smiling broadly, showing neat white teeth. 'Reminds me of Singapore. I was made for this sort of heat; the way it seeps into your bones.'

'You can keep the heat,' said Walker, squinting up into the cloudless sky.

'I was told you spent some time in New Guinea. Didn't you like it?'

He stiffened. 'Wasn't like this,' he muttered.

Angela seemed to get the message that he didn't want to talk about it so she shrugged her delicate shoulders and kept silent until they reached the automatic door into the next building. It failed to open and Walker let out an expletive as he waved his hand at the sensor. Finally, after stepping backwards, the door opened and they went into the relative cool of the darkened corridors that led to the kitchens and service areas of the hospital.

'Angela, are you okay to go up and check the ward? I've got something to do.'

'Of course.'

'Are you sure ... after what happened?'

This time her smile was forced. 'I'm fine.'

'It's understandable if you need time off.' He paused uncertainly. 'Do you have someone to look after you?' He was reluctant to pry and he didn't want her to think he was being forward.

'I'm fine, thank you, Dr Walker.' Her voice was cold. 'I've been caring for myself perfectly well for some years.'

He tried to sound businesslike. 'Of course, of course. Just checking.' They reached a cross-corridor. 'Well, if you are fine with the ward round, I'll see you tomorrow.'

He stared after her, noting how her long lean legs carried her briskly away, then headed off in the opposite direction to the mortuary, feeling like he'd handled the situation badly.

The forensic pathologist, Jocelyn Banks, was an elegant middle-aged woman with neat auburn hair and pearl earrings who had worked at the hospital since it opened in the mid seventies. Western Meadows Hospital had a coroner's court on campus and also a forensic pathology unit, which Dr Banks was part of.

'Find anything?' Walker asked as soon as he arrived. Professor Chee's body was laid out on the stainless-steel mortuary table, his body covered with a sheet and his pallid face appearing serene. Walker had spoken on the phone to Jocelyn that morning after he had tossed and turned all night about the professor's death. She stood before a dull grey computer monitor clicking on the keys with gloved hands.

Jocelyn gave him a knowing smile. 'I'm ahead of you. I'd already sent blood yesterday to the lab and, after your call this morning, I asked them to fast-track the analysis.'

'And?'

'Metoprolol. Lots of it. Enough to kill him.'

'Bloody hell!' gasped Walker. Even though it was he who had suggested the possibility to Jocelyn that morning, he could barely believe it. 'Murder? Who would want to murder Benjamin Chee?'

'Someone did. He wasn't the most popular fellow in the hospital.'

'He was a dickhead, but that's not usually enough for someone to kill you around here.'

Jocelyn snorted. 'Half the surgical department would be dead otherwise.'

Walker feigned astonishment. 'Half the surgical department, Josie? Really, I thought you knew the hospital better than that. I'd estimate at least ninety percent of the surgeons are dickheads.'

She ignored his sarcasm and glanced down at the body. 'Someone wanted him dead though.' She raised her face to Walker. 'I've already called the police at Parramatta station.' A bell rang. 'Speak of the devil, I suspect that'll be them now.'

Detective Sergeant Barry Darling strode into the mortuary, followed by a tall, fresh-faced uniformed policeman who held a peaked cap under his arm. Darling nodded to Jocelyn Banks then looked down at the body on the slab. 'Is this the ...' The question froze in his throat when he glanced up and noticed Walker and his jaw dropped open. 'Kit,' he blurted. 'What are you doing here?'

Jocelyn turned to Walker, who seemed frozen with equal astonishment. 'Kit?' she asked.

Walker ignored her. 'Wendy!'

Jocelyn frowned at the policeman then back at Walker. 'Wendy? What's this all about? You two know each other?'

Walker seemed to be in shock and he spoke mechanically. 'Went to school together.' He looked at Jocelyn then at the corpse, then back at the young officer. 'I've got to go. Ward round,' and he strode out of the room without a backward glance.

Jocelyn stared after him. 'Good friends, are you then?' she asked the policeman sarcastically.

'Used to be,' he said flatly. Seeing Walker was the last thing he had expected. He knew he'd become a doctor but he didn't know he was working at Western Meadows.

*Murder on the Ward*

'Well?' When the officer remained silent, she added, 'I'm not going to call you Wendy. What's your real name?'

Darling forced himself into action and pulled a small spiral-bound pad from his inside pocket. 'Darling,' he said. 'Detective Sergeant Barry Darling, Local Area Command, Parramatta. And this is Senior Constable David Jones.' He indicated the corpse. 'This him?' He looked at his notepad. 'Professor Benjamin Chee?' He looked again at the body. 'You think he was poisoned?'

'No doubt about it. His blood level of metoprolol was through the roof.' When Darling remained blank-faced she added, 'It's a beta-blocker. Used for high blood pressure or heart disease. Or an overactive thyroid, which is what he was in hospital for.'

'Beta-blockers. That's what students take before exams to stop from being nervous.'

Jocelyn nodded. 'Yes, that's right. It slows down your heart rate so you don't feel so anxious. Never worked for me though. But a huge dose stops your heart. That's what I think happened here.'

'You don't say.' Darling tapped his lower lip with his pencil. 'Who would do that? And why?'

'There I can't help you.' She peeled off the surgical gloves. 'I'm stuck in pathology. Never know what's going on in the hospital, except for when a stray surgeon wanders over to complain about my reports.'

'Next of kin then?'

'Angela Chee, his daughter. She's a trainee doctor in the hospital. Working with your friend at the moment, as a matter of fact.' She smiled. 'Kit, I think you called him. We call him Chris Walker. He was the one who suspected foul play and got me to check for the drug in the blood.'

'Walker? What's he got to do with it?'

'Found the body apparently. Along with Angela Chee, the deceased's daughter. Dead in a ward bed. An arrest was called but,' she pointed at the body, 'clearly unsuccessful.'

'The daughter found the body? Along with Chris Walker?'

'That's what I said.'

Darling examined his notes in silence. 'Could the deceased have taken an overdose?'

'Don't think so,' said Jocelyn. 'It was almost certainly given intravenously. There were no empty bottles in the room.'

'Could it have been a mistake by one of the staff then? Wrong drug? Wrong dose?'

She lifted the sheet and pointed to the cannula that still sat in the corpse's arm. 'It was probably administered using that. Look at the bandaging. Sloppy job. Someone inserted that in a hurry.'

Darling tapped on the cover of his notepad with his pencil as if he were playing a small drum. 'Walker found her, hey? And the daughter.' He glanced down at his writing. 'Angela Chee,' he said slowly then looked at Jocelyn thoughtfully. 'Where can I find whoever's in charge around here?'

# CHAPTER SEVEN

WALKER'S EYES CRACKED open. It was Saturday morning. The sun streamed in through open doors that swung to and fro in a cool breeze, a patch of Botticelli-blue sky, washed clean by another night-time storm, visible above a branch of the jacaranda.

He could tell it would be another hot one but the morning breeze promised to delay the onslaught of the summer heat, at least for a little while. He'd spent another sleepless night trying to avoid his dreams and had ended up drifting off in the armchair – Flea's armchair. His neck was sore but, surprisingly, he felt rested. He glanced at the clock on his bedside table – 7:20. He dressed quickly, throwing on an unwashed T-shirt and shorts that he'd worn two days before and discarded on the bedroom floor. Before he left through the front door, he slipped a pair of old sneakers onto his feet.

He loved walking around The Rocks in the morning. The streets were largely devoid of tourists, mostly just locals going about their way, or the occasional late reveller who'd slept in one of the local parks.

The Rocks was the first part of Sydney colonised by a mishmash of convicts and British soldiers with the arrival the First Fleet in 1788. In 1900, a large part was demolished due to an outbreak of the bubonic plague but the original pattern of narrow streets thrown together at odd angles remained. Inexpensive terraces were built to house the waterside workers and most remained, along with a larger number of public drinking houses. Here and there, grand homes and public buildings dating from the first half-century of settlement still stood, mostly built from the local sandstone that gave old Sydney its distinctive appearance.

Walker made his way to the top of Lower Fort and turned left at the Garrison Church onto Argyle Street. He slapped along the footpath down under the great arch of the Argyle Cut, the Saturday morning traffic rumbling overhead as it came off the Harbour Bridge. Up above and to his right was Observatory Park, which housed the original observatory of the colony as well as the school he and Barry Darling had gone to as young children.

At the bottom of Argyle Street, he turned left at the Orient Hotel onto George Street and went into the G'day Café, an old-fashioned milk bar that was open at all hours, and he ordered his usual hamburger.

'Four-fifty, mate,' said the old Arabic gent behind the counter in a broad Australian accent. Walker didn't even raise an eyebrow. The prices in Sydney in 1991 were becoming outrageous as the cost of living soared. However, he could afford it. He owned his terrace, having inherited it from his father. It wasn't worth much but it was home. The premises of The Rocks and Millers Point were mostly council housing and the general populace didn't want to live in the dingy inner suburb, with its rundown terraces and flats perched in the shadow of the Harbour Bridge.

But he loved it. On these streets and alleyways had walked the first settlers of the colony a little over two hundred years ago and he could still feel the history in the buildings and pathways. And the sparkling blue waters of Sydney Harbour, dotted with little islands, was one of the most beautiful views in the world. Plus, the area had some of the best pubs in the city. He could easily have afforded to move somewhere more salubrious but his roots were here. His father and mother. His ancestors. Flea.

Walker crossed George Street and walked down to the water's edge. To his right was the Circular Quay ferry terminal, already busy with yellow and green boats coming and going. Across the glittering, narrow waterway of Circular Quay was the Opera House, the tiled white sails resplendent in the morning sun.

Walker was alone except for the occasional international tourist, their body clocks still set to some other time zone, wandering around waiting for the city to awaken. He chewed on his hamburger watching the Manly ferry powering away, the grunt of the engines throbbing in his chest and the massive propellers churning up the water in its wake. Not far from where he stood, Captain Phillip had dropped his anchor in one of the deepest harbours in the world. Walker finished his breakfast, imagining what it would have been like for the convicts of the First Fleet to have finally stood on the beach within a stone's throw of where he stood now, after a treacherous six-month journey on the high seas. Perhaps it had been a day much like this one?

Later, as he was approaching his home, Walker noticed a white Holden Commodore parked across the street.

Hello, a five-litre V8. A cop car if ever I saw one. And I know the sort of cop who would drive it.

As he approached, Barry Darling stepped out of the car and Walker stopped near his front gate.

'Knew it would be you, Wendy,' Walker called across the road.

Darling looked irritated. 'Don't call me that.'

'Peter Pan then? I like Wendy better.'

'I don't like either.'

Walker rested his hand on the metal front gate. 'What are you doing here then? Visiting your old stamping ground? Seeing who else you can piss off? Thought you said you were never coming back?'

'You know why. The murder.'

Walker looked up and down the street then let out a short breath. 'Come on in then.'

He showed him into a sparsely furnished front room with bare pine timber floors, a cream two-seater lounge and an original cast iron fireplace with a simple timber mantle. Darling sat on the lounge while Walker took up a position beside the empty fireplace. He didn't offer any refreshments.

Barry Darling was wearing an orange polo shirt with blue trousers and leather shoes without socks – casual since it was the weekend but still dressed to impress. Walker had to secretly admit that the bright colours complemented Darling's olive complexion and dark curly hair. He knew he wouldn't get away with those colours with his Celtic colouring.

'Still the snappy dresser, I see,' said Walker.

Darling ignored the comment as he opened his notepad and studied it for a few moments, flicking through the pages as if gathering his thoughts. 'You discovered the deceased?'

'That's right. I called the arrest.'

'Called the arrest?'

'I asked one of the nurses to summon the resuscitation team.'

Darling merely nodded. 'And a Dr Angela Chee was with you at the time?' He looked up. 'The deceased's daughter.'

'Yes,' Walker said. 'We were on a ward round.'

'Seeing your patients.'

'Yes.'

'Was the deceased one of your patients?'

'No.'

'Why were you in his room then? The both of you. On a ward round.'

Walker shrugged. 'I noticed his name on the board and thought I should look in on him. Only polite. He was one of my colleagues.'

Darling scribbled notes as Walker spoke, then paused. '*You* noticed his name.' He said it as if there was something meaningful in it. 'So did his daughter tell you her father was a patient?'

'No.'

Darling raised his head and leaned back. 'Don't you think that's unusual? Her father was in the hospital and it was you who had to discover that he was a patient? What did she say when you indicated you wanted to,' he looked down at his notes, 'look in on him?'

Walker paused then continued warily. 'She said we didn't need to. I suppose she didn't want to bother him.'

'I see.' He scribbled something down then flipped a few pages back. 'Tell me, how did Angela Chee react when you found her father was unconscious?' He looked up. 'Before *you* called the resuscitation team?'

Walker shifted uneasily. 'She was very quiet about it.'

'Quiet?' Darling snapped the word.

'I suppose she was in shock.'

'So she didn't try to resuscitate her father – she *is* a doctor, after all. Or perhaps it was she who ran to call the arrest?'

Walker shook his head stiffly. 'No, I called the arrest by pressing the buzzer. And then I tried to resuscitate him.'

'*You* tried to resuscitate him. Not her?' He glanced at his notes again. 'Tell me how a resuscitation goes.' He smiled. 'I've had to learn it on a dummy, but I've never actually had to do it for real. Take me through a normal resuscitation – say, before the arrest team arrives. What do you do if there are two people?'

Walker let out a tight breath. 'One normally does the chest compression and the other gives mouth-to-mouth.'

'So which did you do?'

'I started chest compression.'

The officer waved his pencil. 'And Angela Chee did the mouth-to-mouth.'

Walker shook his head, blank-faced.

'No?' Darling said in mock surprise. 'So she didn't call for the resuscitation team, she didn't do the chest compression and she didn't do the mouth-to-mouth.' He raised a finger for each point. 'What *did* she do? Just watch her father die?'

When Walker remained silent, Darling continued. 'I understand Angela Chee is a medical registrar training to be a specialist physician.' His lips curled into a fake smile. 'Just like you, Kit. Tell me, when you were at her level of training, how many resuscitations had you done?'

Walker shrugged. 'Maybe fifty.'

Darling pursed his lips in a soundless whistle. 'Fifty. Impressive. And do you suppose she's done that many?'

'I don't know. I suppose so. On after-hours shifts.'

'By then it'd be second nature, wouldn't you agree?'

Walker clamped his jaw. 'Like I said, she was in shock.'

'Like I said, she's a doctor, not some nobody off the street. And it was her father. Double reason to act.'

'She was in shock,' Walker repeated, but this time with no conviction. He knew Darling was right. By the time he'd reached Angela's level of training, resuscitation was a reflex reaction. He'd been there so many times. She should've jumped into action before she knew what she was doing. He wouldn't have frozen, even if it was his own father. *Especially* if it was his father. Something had stopped her. Her failure to act had to be a conscious decision. He looked through the front window then back at Darling. 'I don't think they were very close. He wasn't a very nice man.'

Darling scribbled a note then sat forward on the edge of the lounge. 'You didn't like him either?'

'Not particularly.'

'So his daughter didn't like him and you didn't like him.' He snapped his notepad closed and leaned back again. 'Tell me, what is your relationship with Angela Chee?'

'What do you mean?'

'I'm told she's a very pretty young woman.'

Walker took a step towards him. 'So that's it, is it, Wendy? You're going to frame us both? You and your filthy mind. She is a work colleague, nothing more!' His voice echoed around the small bare room. 'You don't have to try to destroy every woman I come into contact with, you know.'

Darling stood up and pushed his face close to Walker's. 'I don't destroy women, Kit. *You* do, remember?'

Walker wanted to punch his face in. His jaw clamped tight and his fists were two balls shaking at his side. 'Felicity was my wife, Wendy, not yours. Just get over the fact that she loved me, not you.'

'If you loved her so much, why didn't you look after her?' Darling shouted. 'Why is she dead?'

Walker spun away. 'You can piss off, Wendy.'

Darling, breathing heavily, pushed his notepad into his back pocket. 'That'll be enough for now, Kit. But I will need to speak to you again.'

Walker retreated to the fireplace and stared at the empty grate. 'Don't call me that. Only my old friends called me that.' He turned. "And don't come here again. If you want to see me, make an appointment at the hospital.'

He watched through the window as Darling crossed the street to his car. Darling paused, key in hand, and examined a large Edwardian building opposite, used as a nursing home – Darling House – the place that had given the police officer his name.

Soon afterwards, Walker heard the rumble of the V8 as his former friend drove away.

Deep in thought, he made his way through the back door of the terrace and sat on an old timber chair in the shade. The tiny backyard had a brick wall shared with the adjacent terrace on one side and, on the other, an old timber lean-to, which served as an outdoor laundry. The ground was cracked concrete, devoid of plants except for a few weeds around the edges. He knew he really should do something about it – that, and the rest of the house – but with Felicity gone, he couldn't see the point. At the back was a set of concrete stairs that went up to a flimsy timber gate set in the rear fence. On the stairs, a huge shaggy ginger cat was curled up in a ball, sunning himself.

Walker's chair scraped as he sat down, which triggered a voice from the backyard of the terrace on his right.

'That you, Chris?' It was his neighbour, her voice coarse from heavy smoking. 'Is Archie with you?'

'He's here, Janet,' called Walker over the fence, not bothering to move. 'Asleep on the back step.'

'Send him back when he wakes up, will you, love? I need to worm him.'

'Sure, Janet.'

A head appeared over the top of the fence; wild orange hair on a tanned, wrinkled face. 'I saw Barry Darling just now,' said Janet. 'Haven't seen him for years. Whatever happened to you two? Used to be thick as thieves.' She gave a hoarse chuckle. 'In fact, if I'm not mistaken, you *were* thieves. A lot of videos and TVs went astray when you two were knocking around, including mine, if my memory serves me correctly.' She sucked back on a cigarette and blew out the smoke through tight lips. 'I hear he's a copper now.' She let out a chuckle. 'Trying to atone for his sins maybe?'

'Maybe,' Walker said, trying to sound disinterested. 'Don't know. Don't care.'

'Bullshit. You two were the best of friends. What happened? Is it about Felicity?'

He let out an emotionless laugh. 'Maybe. He's a total dickhead. Could never get over Flea loving me rather than him.'

Her eyes bored into him. He looked away and began to scratch his foot. 'Chris, I think you two should try to make up. Life is hard enough without ditching your best friends along the way.' He refused to meet her gaze. 'Family and close friends,' she persisted. 'That's all we have to stick up for us in the end.' Her head disappeared. 'Anyway, enough said. Send Archie in when you can.'

He heard the slam of the fly-screen door and sat staring at the cat, thinking about what had just happened.

Walker and Barry Darling had been the closest of friends, closer than brothers, and had grown up together. Darling had lived across the road in Darling House, left on the doorstep as a baby, and by some quirk of the law that Walker had never understood had been raised by the owners of the nursing home – or rather by the nurses, who saw it as their responsibility to care for the child.

Darling had little parental supervision, and neither did Walker. His father was a widower and worked long hours on the docks, so when they were young, the two boys roamed the streets getting up to all sorts of shenanigans.

The 'Disney Twins', the locals used to call them, a totally inaccurate description, in his opinion. Barry Darling had got his nickname from the book *Peter Pan* by J.M Barrie, which had nothing to do with Walt Disney. The children in the book had the surname Darling. Sometimes Barry was called Peter Pan, but mostly Wendy after the older sister.

And it was Darling who first linked his favourite comic book character with Walker. Darling had turned up at his place early one morning when he was about fourteen, all in a lather, after he'd discovered that Christopher 'Kit' Walker was also the name of the Phantom. After that was out, the locals couldn't help themselves. For a while they were the Dynamic Duo. But one day the local copper, Sergeant Bowles, who had yet again hauled them up to the cop shop for a break-and-enter charge and was threatening detention, had christened them the Disney Twins. The name had stuck.

Walker sat in the shade, lost in the memory of their childhood together, full of fun, mischief and adventure. But it had all turned sour over a local girl – Felicity Bedford; Flea, they called her. They had both loved her but, in the end, Walker had won her heart. But that wasn't what caused their falling out – it was Flea's death and the circumstances surrounding it. Barry had never forgiven him. Walker dug his knuckles into his forehead trying to forget, feeling the pain – physical pain – much easier than the awful ragged cut that tore at his soul.

Walker felt something furry rub against his leg. Archie had woken and now wanted some attention. He picked him up, grunting with the weight. Archie was a fully grown Siberian and weighed over eight kilograms. Walker lifted him onto his lap, stretched the furry bundle along his legs and proceeded to scratch the cat's neck and belly while Archie purred, a little motor deep in his chest, sounding like a small lion.

When he had finished, Walker heaved him up onto his chest as if he was a baby and stood up.

'Come on, Archie. Time for you to go home. Time to get wormed.'

# CHAPTER EIGHT

ANGELA MET WALKER in his office and waited patiently outside while he finished dictating a letter about a patient on his hand-held dictaphone. Walker studied her out of the corner of his eye, her head bowed reading a journal article as she waited. She wore a tight black skirt and a snug floral top that was cut away at the shoulders, and black flats – all best quality, as far as he could tell.

When he finished, he gave her a wave. He hadn't informed her that her father had been murdered and he wondered whether Darling had yet got to her. She looked calm enough, but based on her reactions of the last few days, that didn't mean anything. He decided he'd leave it to the cops and not mention it. He felt like a coward but he figured it was probably the right protocol anyway.

She smiled when he stood up. 'Good morning, Dr Walker.'

'Hi, Angela. Are you all right?'

'Fine, thank you. Shall we do a round?'

The walked along the carpeted air bridge that connected the clinical building to the ward block. The air bridge leaked when it rained and the carpet smelled musty.

As they reached the stairwell that led to the wards above, Angela spoke. 'I have some bad news. The admission from last night has died. Found dead by the nursing staff early this morning.'

'That's too bad,' said Walker. He noticed she didn't complain when he took the stairs rather than the lift. They had five flights to climb and Walker took every opportunity to exercise. He raised his eyebrows. 'Was an arrest called?'

Her black ponytail, held in place by a red ribbon, flicked from side to side when she shook her head. 'She was cold when they found her. Her lung cancer was fairly advanced.'

'What did she die from?'

'Pneumonia, I think.'

They had reached the fourth floor and Walker noticed that Angela wasn't puffing despite doing most of the talking. It was a trick that one of his old bosses had taught him when he was a registrar. A fitness fanatic, his old boss used to make his team run up the stairs of the hospital while doing rounds, getting the residents to present cases at the same time so they would arrive puffing and sweating at the top. Walker now tried to do the same; not to be nasty, he just considered it a nice tradition. However, to his mild irritation, Angela had not even worked up a sweat and, after taking a few deep breaths when they reached the top, she was soon breathing normally.

Fit too, he thought to himself. Wonder when she exercises? He idly imagined her in a tight black leotard stretched over firm buttocks, low cut at the front to show the top of taut breasts.

'The patient's relatives have consented to an autopsy.'

He snapped out of his reverie. 'Autopsy? What for?'

'Dr Walker, it is the policy of our department to get an autopsy when we can. How will we ever learn to help our other patients?'

Walker cleared his throat. 'Of course. It's just that most junior docs find it uncomfortable asking.'

'I don't.'

'Good to see,' he said. Then after a pause he added, 'Well done.'

They reached the nurses' station, the centre of the horseshoe crowded with nurses and residents, talking and laughing, signing charts and undertaking other duties. Among them was Gloria, Walker's intern, orange-haired with a permanently startled face. She was talking to the skinny, bespectacled exchange student from Kuala Lumpur with the unfortunate name of Sandy Fuk. He had been working with them for four months and was proving to be a useful addition, doing a lot of the intern's work, and often more efficiently.

Walker had initially tried to politely discourage Sandy from using his anglicised name but changed his mind when offered the alternative of his Chinese name – Fuk Yee-Hah. Now everyone just called him Sandy or Dr Sandy, except Angela, who called him Yee-Hah.

'What do you think the autopsy will show?' Walker asked Angela now.

'I think the clinical picture is one of pneumonia.'

'Hmm. What about the chest X-ray?'

'Fairly clear, but the signs of pneumonia take a few days to show.'

'What about pulmonary embolism?'

'I don't think so,' she said quickly – a little too quickly in Walker's opinion. It wasn't good to be so definite. He thought he should teach her a lesson.

'Wanna bet?'

'What?'

'Do you want to bet on it? A wager?'

'I know what a bet is,' she said, unsuccessfully hiding her irritation. To Walker's satisfaction, she also looked uncertain. 'So you want to place a bet that it was an embolism, not an infection?'

'Pneumonia,' corrected Walker, then raised his arms magnanimously. 'But, okay, let's say infection.'

She picked up the bundle of the deceased patient's notes, flicked through the pathology results and studied the electrocardiograph. When she looked up, her expression was firm. 'What's the wager?'

Walker pursed his lips. Dinner perhaps? Then – Don't be stupid, her father's just been murdered. 'A cup of coffee. A proper one at Mrs Marshal's across the road.'

'Big stakes,' she said. Then she smiled and thrust out her hand. 'Agreed.'

Walker shook her hand. Soft and warm. 'Agreed.'

Sandy, who had witnessed the whole conversation, scratched his nose and pushed back his glasses, then straightened them again and shook his head. 'Bad habit, you know.' He had the staccato lilt of Malaysian English. 'I studied this at university. Many Chinese have ruined their lives from gambling.' He shook his head again. 'Very bad habit.'

'It's just a cup of coffee, Yee-Hah,' said Angela, although Walker noticed she seemed embarrassed.

'Thin end of the wedge,' announced Sandy, raising a single index finger.

'Tell me about the patients, Sandy,' Walker interrupted to change the topic.

The student proceeded to deliver a succinct summary of all the patients, including their diagnoses, investigation results, any treatment instituted and their discharge plan. Walker was impressed. Gloria the intern, who was supposed to be supervising the student, merely added information at various points on Sandy's bidding. Strangely, she seemed content with the situation, treating him more like a senior colleague than an underling. Walker had the feeling she'd be floundering if it were not for Sandy.

Sandy led the way but stopped abruptly, causing Walker to almost run into him. Andy Korbmann, the wardsman, was idly leaning against the end of the nurses' station. He was tall and thin with greying hair and a beak of a nose. He'd been a permanent fixture at the hospital for years and most of the staff knew him.

'You will let me practise my cannulation on you today, Andy?' asked Sandy.

## Murder on the Ward

'Sure,' said Andy. 'And you can teach me some Malay. I'll be going to KL for a holiday later this year and it will come in handy.'

'No problem. I'll teach you perfect Malay. The locals will be amazed. It will get you best price when you are bargaining.'

Walker was about to tell Sandy to get moving when Gloria interrupted. 'Come on, Sandy.' She sounded irritated. 'Dr Walker will want you to present the patients.'

Walker thought she was being uncharacteristically forceful. Mostly she spoke only when asked a question.

'See you later,' called Sandy to the wardsman as Jenny joined the group, and they moved away to start the round.

'We'll have to stop meeting like this,' said Jocelyn Banks. 'People will start thinking you have a thing for me.'

Walker couldn't tell whether she was smiling behind her blue mask. Jocelyn stood leaning against a counter with her arms folded across her chest, swathed in blue linens and wearing a long white plastic apron, as she waited for the technician to open the chest of the body that lay on the stainless-steel bench before them. Walker and Angela stood back to ensure none of the blood or tissue hit them as Johnson, the bald, elderly pathology assistant, cut along the ribs on both sides with a large pair of shears. Jocelyn had already made the initial incision through the skin – Y-shaped on the chest and then a single incision down the front of the abdomen to the pubic bone – and had pulled the skin and tissue of the chest up over the head to expose the ribcage.

'We'll open the chest first,' said Jocelyn. 'That should give you your answer. Then I can get rid of you. I've a pile of reports to do upstairs and my registrar has called in sick so I have to do this.' Her eyes flashed meaningfully to Angela Chee as if it were her fault, which of course it was, since Angela had ordered the autopsy.

Johnson finished the job then Jocelyn took a scalpel to the diaphragm and other tissue so the chest wall could be taken away. With the chest cavity now open, Walker and Angela stepped forward. The heart lay in the middle of the chest and slightly to the left, and greyish pink sponge-like tissue filled the rest of the space. Between the lungs ran the tube-like structures that were the blood vessels.

'Thanks, Johnson,' Jocelyn murmured as she peered in. 'Hmm,' she said, swinging the scalpel in a short arc with her fingers in feigned puzzlement. 'Embolism or infection.' She glanced up at Walker. 'What's riding on this?'

'A cup of coffee,' said Walker. 'What can you see?'

'A cup of coffee! Big spenders. I can't see anything yet,' she said. 'I have to examine the lungs.'

'Well, don't let us hold you up, Jocelyn. We all have work to do.' Walker had intended to be light-hearted but realised he sounded short.

'Steady on, Chris,' said Jocelyn. Walker was certain she made a face behind her mask. 'It's just that it's such a huge wager, I wanted to make sure.' Mask or no mask, that was sarcasm if he'd ever heard it.

'Take your time,' he answered with equal sarcasm.

'Let's cut to the chase then.' She proceeded to briskly open the large pulmonary vein, cutting from left to right. Inside a large reddish-black clot straddled across both sides.

'Saddle embolism,' Angela sighed.

'Looks like you owe Dr Walker a cup of coffee, Dr Chee,' Jocelyn said smugly.

'Is there any infection at all?' asked Angela.

Jocelyn squeezed the lungs gently, first the left and then the right. 'Don't think so. Won't know for sure until we cut them open.'

Angela stepped away glumly. 'Thanks, Dr Banks.'

As they left the mortuary, Angela said, 'Guess I owe you a cup of coffee.'

Before he could answer, Walker saw Detective Darling and his sidekick making their way towards them along the dim service corridor littered with broken beds and other apparatus. While they were still a fair way off, Walker stopped and faced his registrar. 'Angela, I think the detective is here to speak to you. He'll have news of your father.'

She frowned at the approaching policeman. 'News?'

'Just remember, I'm here to help if you need me.'

She turned back to Walker, her face questioning. 'Help? What for?'

'Dr Chee,' Darling called out before he reached them. 'If you have a few minutes I need to ask you some questions.' Without waiting for her to answer, he continued. 'Is there somewhere private where we can talk?'

Walker watched them walk away together, uncertain how he should feel. He should be sorry for her, but she didn't seem sad in the least about losing her sole surviving parent. And she'd acted quite unnaturally when she found her father dead in the hospital bed. Still, he couldn't believe she had anything to do with his death. But then he began to question that feeling. Why did he think that? Could he be influenced by the fact he felt attracted to her? He was lonely, and he had the sense that she was lonely too. He didn't really know anything about her except that she was clever, born in Singapore and seemed to be a very efficient doctor.

He decided he'd have to leave it up to his former friend, Barry Darling, to find out the truth.

'Wendy,' he murmured to himself. 'You stupid dick.' If it wasn't for Flea, they'd probably still be best friends. Where did it all go wrong? But as hard as he tried, he could not remember any specific incident that had caused their friendship to dissolve. Flea choosing him over Darling had certainly started it, but he couldn't actually remember arguing with Darling about it. Their friendship had just slowly unravelled and died, leaving a nubbin of emotion – an emotion that had been difficult to identify at the time.

And now his wife was dead, he didn't know what to think. After Flea died, Darling had come to him, but not to commiserate. He had been furious, accusing Walker of not looking after her. Worse, he'd blamed Walker for her death.

And Walker knew he was right.

# CHAPTER NINE

IT WAS AFTER five and Walker sat at his desk reading the December issue of the *Journal of Clinical Oncology*, freshly arrived and just out of the wrapper. In it was an editorial about monoclonal antibodies – 'magic bullets' the popular press called them – that were supposed to specifically target cancer.

What a pipedream, he thought as he finished the article and flicked to the next page. If anything ever comes of that rubbish, I'll eat my hat.

The pager on his belt beeped and he frowned down at the unfamiliar number, then picked up his phone and stabbed the buttons.

'Dr Walker, thanks for answering. This is Sanjeev, one of the pharmacists.'

Walker thought he recognised his voice – a squat pharmacist who had worked in oncology the previous year.

'Why yes, Sanjeev. What can I do for you?' He couldn't imagine why the pharmacist would be calling him.

His voice was low and strained. 'It's about Professor Chee. I wonder whether we can meet. There is something not right.'

'Professor Chee?' Walker wondered whether Sanjeev had found out about the metoprolol. He remembered him more clearly now, a clever but quiet Indian chap. Or maybe he was Sri Lankan – Walker was never sure.

The fact that Chee's death was a murder had not yet been publicly announced but Walker thought Sanjeev must have figured it out. Maybe he'd found the empty ampoules. 'Sure, Sanjeev. Have you found something?'

'Yes, yes,' came the muted reply over the phone. 'It does not seem right.'

'Okay. Do you want to come to my office?'

'No!' Walker had to strain to hear the hissed reply. 'Meet me down on level one, out the back. In the docks behind D block. I have to show you something.'

'When?'

'Now.' Then a pause. 'Fifteen minutes.'

Walker hung up, deep in thought as he drummed his fingers on the desktop. He opened the top drawer – there, in a plastic bag normally used for transporting blood specimens, was the stub of the ampoule he'd found next to Chee's corpse. He felt guilty that he hadn't given it to Darling but he couldn't bring himself to contact him after their run-in a few days before. He promised himself he'd hand it in the next time he saw him, so he stuck the plastic bag into the pocket of his jacket.

He figured he'd head straight home after he spoke to Sanjeev, so he made a quick check of his in-tray, and swore when he saw a pile of letters that needed signing.

'How did you get there?' he grunted. He was sure the secretaries sneaked into his room when he wasn't looking to pile up his chores at the end of the day.

He huddled over the pages, speed-reading them, and signing them in an irritated scrawl. Halfway through the pile, he calmed himself and continued in a more dignified manner. The referring GPs had a hard enough job without having to contend with a petulant oncologist. When he glanced at his watch, he saw with a start that over twenty-five minutes had gone by.

'Damn!' He jumped up, grabbed his bag and rushed out without locking his door, leaving it to the cleaners who would come later.

He hurried down the stairs and along the drab grey linoleum-covered corridor to the back of the hospital and the docks that received the daily shipments. At this time of day, the docks were empty and the roller doors locked down. The lights were dim, leaving only enough illumination to safely navigate around the stacks of crates and pallets. At the other end of the dock, in a dark corner, Walker could see the red lights of a forklift and hear the purr of the gas-powered motor. Someone was obviously working late.

He looked up and down the storage area and then at his watch. It was after six. Perhaps Sanjeev had left when Walker hadn't come on time.

He decided he'd wait another five minutes then make tracks. He could already taste the cool schooner that was waiting for him on the bar at the Hero.

The forklift was still in the same spot, the motor grumbling and the headlights lighting up the besser block wall at the end of the docks. As far as Walker could see, there was no one driving it. He used to work in Flemington Markets when he was a medical student, stacking fruit during the Christmas season, so he knew something about the machines. No self-respecting operator would leave a forklift running while not at the controls. He wandered towards it with some reluctance. Maybe the driver had suffered a stroke or a heart attack.

'There goes my beer,' he muttered. But when he reached the truck, there was no driver slumped over the controls as expected. Irritated, he looked around.

'Dickhead!' He moved to turn off the engine, but as he leaned into the cab, he saw it. Wedged up against the wall, skewered by one blade of the fork, was the body of a man. Walker didn't have to check the pulse to know he was dead. The fork had penetrated his chest and splayed his ribs apart, dissecting the large vessels in his chest. His face was white and lifeless, mouth slack, and on the floor beneath him was a large puddle of blood. More blood streamed down the wall behind the body like a small river.

Walker recognised him.
Sanjeev, the pharmacist.


Barry Darling frowned down at the pool of blood at his feet with a look of intense distaste, as if someone had made a mess in his kitchen. Then he turned his attention to Walker, who stood on the other side of the forklift cab away from the body and next to the burly Constable Jones. Police tape had been set across the crime scene and several people dressed in plain clothes were buzzing around, measuring and collecting samples. A young woman, who to Walker's eyes looked like a teenager, was dusting the forklift steering wheel with powder.

'So *you* found him.' Darling transferred his attention from the pool of blood to Walker. He stepped out of the way to let a crime scene officer take photos of the body and crossed to Walker. 'What the hell are you up to, Kit? I thought you were a bloody oncologist trying to save lives, not collecting dead bodies.'

He shrugged. 'Not my fault, Wendy. I didn't kill him. He wanted to meet me.'

'Meet you? What for? Why down here?'

'He said he had information about Chee's death. He said there was something not right.'

'Of course there was something not right. He was bloody well murdered.'

'He didn't know that. I thought he'd found empty metoprolol ampoules.'

'If you thought that, you should have called me straightaway.' He moved towards Walker. 'So you're sick of being a doctor now, is that it, Kit? You want to be a detective instead?'

'No, Wendy. Sanjeev sounded tense. And I was in a hurry.' Walker looked around sheepishly to check who was listening and he dropped his voice. 'I wanted to get home.'

'Home? Keen to get up to the Hero for a beer, you mean.'

Now it was Darling's turn to look over at the cluster of onlookers who stood near the door that led into the main hospital – mostly kitchen staff and a few nurses. 'Move them away, will you, Jones?'

Using his considerable bulk, Jones waved the small crowd away into the hospital building and closed the door, allowing the investigation team privacy.

As Jones made his way back, Darling turned back to Walker. 'Where's your little girlfriend, Chee's daughter? Is she in on this as well? Are you both roaming around like the dynamic duo or something?' He smirked. 'Ha! Or the Boy Wonder and Astro Girl, more like it.'

Constable Jones joined him with a laugh.

Walker ignored them. 'I don't know where she is. And she's not my girlfriend, she's my registrar. Purely professional.'

Darling huffed. 'Come off it, Kit. I know you. You were always of the Asian persuasion.'

'Piss off, Wendy.'

Darling lowered his voice and moved closer. 'What I don't understand is why you married Flea. Blonde and Aussie. Not really your type.'

Walker bunched his fists by his side. 'That's totally inappropriate, Wendy.' He kept his voice tight and low. 'Anyway, she loved me, Wendy, not you. Just get over it.'

'Great lot of good it did her,' he hissed. 'You didn't look after her very well, did you? Look where she is now.' Darling appeared as if he immediately regretted what he just said. But before he could move, Walker launched himself at the detective and gave him a sharp right hook onto the side of his head. Darling shouted and raised his arms but Walker caught him with an undercut with his left fist.

'Aggh!' barked Darling and shoved Walker away, allowing Jones to grab him around the chest.

'You're a bloody arse,' shouted Walker.

'You're the arse, Kit,' grunted Darling. He held his nose and leaned forward to allow blood to drip onto the ground.

Jones kicked Walker's legs out from beneath him so he landed on his knees, then moved his hold up around his neck. 'You're dead meat, you little wimp,' he growled as he tightened his grip.

'Lucky you're as weak as piss, Kit.' Darling moved to the policeman and placed a restraining arm on his shoulder. 'Let him go, Jones. He's not worth it. He didn't hurt me.'

Jones held his grip around Walker's neck, whose face was now engorged, his mouth wide open as he struggled for air. The forensic team had stopped work and were staring at them.

'I said let him go,' insisted Darling. 'I've done worse to him in the past.'

With a disgruntled look, Jones released his arms to allow Walker to fall forward on all fours onto the concrete dock, his chest heaving.

Darling stood over him. 'Go home, Kit. We'll speak about this later. Come and see me at the station in the morning.'

As Walker pulled himself unsteadily to his feet, Darling added, 'And try not to find any more bodies.'

# CHAPTER TEN

WALKER DROPPED IN at the Parramatta police station just after eight in the morning and was somewhat surprised to learn from the clerk that Darling was already there. She led him up to his office on the second floor.

Walker had decided he should give the detective the glass ampoule he'd found on Chee's bed but he didn't want to endure the derision he was sure Darling would give him for the delayed delivery. He'd been counting on his memory of Barry Darling being a late starter and hoped he'd miss him, especially since their tussle the night before.

Darling sat at his desk dressed in a tight grey suit and a wide floral orange tie that blended with his swarthy skin. His nose was slightly swollen but not as much as Walker thought it should be after the punch he'd given him. Disconcerted, Walker wondered whether he was losing his touch.

To his surprise, the detective didn't even mention their fight and merely glanced at the ampoule stub after Walker had given it to him, then placed it on the desktop. 'You think this is important?' he said with disinterest.

'Could be. It was next to Professor Chee's body.'

'So? It's a hospital. There must be loads of these things lying around. There was a resuscitation.'

Walker was irritated at his off-hand manner. 'It was on the wrong side of the body. And it doesn't look familiar. I'm sure it isn't an adrenalin ampoule.'

'What then?'

'I don't know. I haven't memorised all the different ampoules. There's hundreds of them.'

'Why bring it now then if you think it's important?'

Walker let out a breath. Here it comes, he thought. Some sort of smart-arse comment.

But instead, Darling shrugged his shoulders. 'Okay, I'll get it checked out.' He pushed it to the side of his desk. 'You at the hospital today? I'll be seeing the head of pharmacy and I want you to come along.'

'Me? What for?'

'All the medical mumbo-jumbo. You might be useful. Saves me looking things up.'

'I should be free later in the morning if that suits.' Then he changed tack. 'What do you think of Sanjeev? Do you have any idea who killed him?'

'I was about to ask you the same thing.'

'No idea. But as I said, I think he had some clue about who the murderer might be.'

'And so he was killed to stop telling you?'

'Looks like it.'

'Wow, Kit, is that how you work in medicine? Two plus two equals ten? We have to go on more than hunches in the force, you know. Or the Police *Service,* as we're now called.' Darling rolled his eyes at the last.

Walker thought about leaving but he had the feeling Darling wanted to talk, so he ventured a question he had been mulling over all night. 'Wendy, do you still think Angela killed her father? I doubt very much that she can drive a forklift.'

'Who said I thought she'd killed him?' Darling frowned at him with mock surprise. 'Anyway, I like to keep an open mind, Kit. This is the time of women's rights, remember. They can do anything a man can do apparently. Even drive a forklift!'

'Give me a break, Wendy.'

'Anyway, the truth'll come out eventually. The killer will make a mistake. They always do. Or someone will talk.' Darling smiled wryly. 'You know what they say – "The Phantom has a thousand eyes and a thousand ears."'

Walker shook his head. 'You still doing that Phantom stuff, Wendy?' He raised his eyebrows. 'You still got your rings?'

Darling's eyes flicked to his top drawer then back to Walker. 'And you haven't? That vow we made was real as far as I'm concerned.'

Walker let out a short laugh. 'What? So you punch the baddies with your skull ring to mark them?'

Darling paused before answering. 'Sometimes. Yeah, sometimes I do.'

'You're kidding, aren't you?'

Darling remained silent and frowned down at the desktop, flicking a pencil in an arc between his fingers. Walker studied him. Maybe his old friend really believed he *was* the Phantom. He was olive-skinned with dark, tight hair and a strong nose, and Walker had to admit there was a certain regal, Mediterranean look about him. Although Darling had no knowledge of his parents, there was no doubt he was of Mediterranean extraction. Italian maybe, or even Spanish.

Finally, Darling looked up from below dark, knitted eyebrows. 'Kit, we have to talk about what happened to Flea.'

Walker stirred uncomfortably in his chair. 'Why? What's that got to do with anything?' His words were brusque and he felt angry that his former friend had brought up the subject, but at the same time guilty that he felt angry about it. Flea had been Darling's friend as well as his before she became his wife. Darling probably loved her at one time – maybe still did. But Walker wasn't ready to talk about it now, or maybe ever. Just thinking about her threatened to open the chasm in his chest.

'How did she die in New Guinea?'

'I said I don't want to talk about it.'

'I heard she drowned,' Darling persisted, 'but I've never heard the details.'

'You investigating her death too, Wendy? Investigating me? There were never any charges laid.'

'Charges,' said Darling with honest surprise. 'Why would there be charges?' His eyes were now penetrating. 'Chris, tell me what happened. Why would there be charges?'

Walker stood abruptly. 'Nothing happened. It was just a horrible accident. I almost died too, you know. I was in la-la land for months.'

'Where, Chris? What do you mean? Where were you?'

'You already know. The highlands of New Guinea. Southeast of Mount Hagen.' Walker closed his eyes and struggled to calm his breathing. Finally, he opened his eyes again. 'It was an accident. She drowned. That's all you need to know. You just have to believe me.' Walker moved towards the door. 'I have a clinic I'm late for.' He opened the door and left quickly on shaky legs.

After Walker left, Darling sat staring at the door for some moments. Finally, he stirred, picked up the phone and dialled a number. 'Debbie, put me through to the Feds in Port Moresby, please.'

'The PNG government?'

'No, the Australian Federal Police. There must be some sort of liaison officer.'

There was a pause before she replied. 'We don't seem to have a liaison officer.'

'What do mean we don't have one? It's bloody Port Moresby. We only gave them independence fifteen years ago, there must be someone.'

'Not since the Treaty on Development Cooperation, apparently. I can find out for you, but it will take a bit of time.'

'Thanks, Deb. Please let me know when you find out.' He slammed the phone down. 'Treaty on Development Cooperation, my arse. Development Confusion more likely.'

He picked up the plastic bag that Walker had given him and looked closely at the glass stub with the yellow band. 'Probably another bloody red herring, Kit, you stupid dick.' He stuffed it into the pocket of his jacket.


Walker felt distracted and irritated in his clinic that morning and, unaccountably, he was short with his registrar and snapped at her a few times when she seemed to be taking too long with the patients. 'Hurry up, Angela. We don't have the luxury to natter all day with the patients. We're not bloody psychiatrists. I don't want to have to do this whole clinic myself.' He immediately regretted his words since he realised, she wasn't going slow, at all.

But instead of being curt in return, as she was entitled to, she lowered her eyes demurely, apologised and promised to speed up.

Walker felt ashamed and the next time Angela asked about a patient, he tried to be more supportive.

'It's Belinda,' she said. 'She's finished her chemo and wants to know where we go from here.'

'Are the tumour markers normal?'

Angela nodded. 'AFP is two and beta-HCG is undetectable.'

'Good,' said Walker. 'Let's talk to her together.'

Belinda was still totally bald but had retained her eyebrows. Now that she was out of hospital and wearing normal clothes, she looked healthy and attractive despite her alopecia, having regained the colour in her face.

'You're looking well, Belinda,' Walker said with a smile. 'A bit like Sinead O'Connor.' O'Connor's rendition of 'Nothing Compares 2 U' had been playing on the radio almost continuously lately, and although seeing her shaved head on TV may not have made bald women exactly fashionable, it had allowed many of the cancer patients to be brave enough not to bother with wigs.

'Do you still have any side effects?' asked Walker.

'Well, this obviously,' she rubbed her hand over her scalp, 'but now I've got numbness in my feet. Like I'm walking on cotton wool.' Her brow furrowed. 'Do you think it's anything serious?'

'The hair will start growing back now – about one centimetre a month, but it might be curly and darker initially. Eventually it will go back to normal. The numbness in your feet is from the cisplatin. I remember telling you that you might get it but you probably forgot.' He smiled. 'Too much to know. It often comes on after the chemo and people worry that it's the cancer coming back. The good news is that it usually gets better when it's due to cisplatin, unlike some other drugs. But it takes a long time, maybe a year. Nerves take forever to heal.'

'That's good to know,' said Belinda. 'So, where to from here?'

'Well, there is an excellent chance you are cured. The markers are normal and we managed to get all the treatment in on time and in a good dose. So now we just wait. The longer we go on without a recurrence the more likely you are to be cured.'

Belinda smiled and breathed an exaggerated sigh of relief. 'So it's not been a waste of time having all those side effects.'

'I don't think so. How about you come back in a few weeks for a CT scan? That should be clear and then we'll start the follow-up phase.'

After Belinda had left, Angela presented another patient, a forty-four-year-old businessman who'd recently had surgery for testicular cancer. 'It's stage one,' said Angela. 'Markers are normal, as is the CT scan.'

'Did you look at it yourself?'

'Yes, but I wouldn't mind you checking it.' She pointed to the films on the viewer.

'Which side testicle was it?' asked Walker.

'Right.'

Walker carefully reviewed the films, paying special attention to the lymph nodes that ran along the major artery and vein in the abdomen between the kidneys. 'Looks clear to me. Where is he?'

Walker introduced himself to Aaron Young, who sat in the clinic room with his wife. He seemed fairly laid-back for a man newly diagnosed with cancer. Walker didn't want to repeat the history and examination of his registrar but felt it important to ask a few questions to establish rapport.

'Have you got over the operation all right?'

'Yes,' said Aaron, then paused thoughtfully. 'Although there was one thing I didn't mention to your assistant here. I think I might have had a reaction to the anaesthetic or something. I keep smelling this funny odour at odd times. It lasts half an hour or so then goes. But Maria can't smell it.' He tilted his head towards his wife.

'Blocked drains?' asked Walker with a smile.

'No, as I mentioned, Maria can't smell it and it happens in different parts of the house. Last night I smelled it coming down the stairs from the bedrooms.'

'And another thing,' his wife added, 'I think the anaesthetic has done something to his brain. I've found him a few times just sitting in the lounge room with a dumb look on his face. He doesn't answer me for a minute or so, then it's like a switch comes on and he returns to the land of the living.'

Walker frowned. 'Doesn't sound like the anaesthetic. Not sure what it is though. Perhaps we should just see how it goes. Your tests are all clear so you have a stage one cancer. But we need to keep an eye on you. If the cancer comes back, we can cure it with chemotherapy, unlike most other cancers.'

Aaron winced. 'Don't like the sound of that. Nasty stuff. My uncle died from it. He had cancer in his liver but was in pretty good shape. He started chemotherapy and the weight just fell off him; he only lasted six months. I think it was the chemo that killed him.'

Walker resisted the temptation to say that almost certainly the weight loss was due to progressive cancer, not the chemotherapy, but decided he didn't have the time to get into a long discussion. They still had six patients to see.

'Well, let's hope we never need it. Can we see you again in two months with another CT scan and blood tests? The risk of relapse, if it happens, is greatest in the first two years.'

'And what's the chance of that happening?'

Walker flicked through the pathology report again. 'Well, it's embryonal carcinoma – a type of testis cancer – and there is no evidence of tumour cells in the blood vessels.' He looked up at the patient. 'The risk is only about fifteen percent.'

'Only!' said Aaron. 'That sounds high.'

'Which is why you need to turn up for your visits and have all the tests.'

'I'll make sure he does, Dr Walker,' said his wife, grabbing her husband's hand.

'Okay,' said Walker, giving them a reassuring smile. 'I'll see you in two months.'

## CHAPTER ELEVEN

WALKER AND DARLING were led through the glass security door and shown into the office of the Director of Pharmacy. Maisie Diver was about their age with an unremarkable face but was the sort that could have posed as a body double in the bedroom scene of a blockbuster movie, although she seemed completely unaware of her charms. She wore a plain, shapeless shift that failed to hide her curves and she smiled widely when she greeted them.

'Good morning, Chris. And this would be Detective Darling.' Her voice was smooth and strong. 'It's terrible news about Sanjeev. Please, take a seat.'

Walker noticed how Darling stared at her body as she smoothly moved to the other side of the desk to take her own chair.

Maisie shook her head. 'Why would anyone want to kill Sanjeev?'

'Dr Walker here thinks Sanjeev found out something about Professor Chee. Something suspicious.'

She looked from face to face. 'But what?'

'We thought you might be able to help.'

'I'll help in any way I can. What would you like to know?'

'What department was Sanjeev assigned to?'

'Anaesthetics.'

'Did he have anything to do with the ward where Professor Chee died?'

'No. He was mostly involved with the restocking of the anaesthetic drugs for theatres. That's a pretty busy job. He wouldn't have had time to go up to the wards.'

'Can you think of anything he might have come across that would have made him suspicious?'

'Like what?'

'Professor Chee received a very high dose of metoprolol into the vein, enough to kill him. Perhaps Sanjeev came across empty ampoules somewhere.'

Maisie Diver frowned in thought. 'I can't imagine where,' she said slowly. 'Unless it was down here in the department.'

'Could someone have got in here and stolen a supply?'

'This is a secure area. You need a pass card to enter unless you're let in, like you were just now. But even then, you need to swipe your pass card again to get into the formulary. Only pharmacists have access.'

Darling jotted down a few lines in his notepad then flicked back a few pages before looking up. 'Where was Sanjeev working on the day he died?'

Both men's eyes ran up and down her feminine curves as Maisie stood and bent over to open the bottom drawer of a grey metal filing cabinet. She pulled out a wad of typed A4 sheets. 'One day we'll computerise these, I suppose, but I still do the rosters on paper.' She flicked to the second page and ran a finger down it. When she turned to them, both men's eyes snapped up to her face. 'He was restocking the endoscopy unit.'

'Is metoprolol used there?' asked Darling.

'Hardly ever,' said Maisie. 'It's not a stock item in the endoscopy unit.'

'What then?'

'Narcotics and benzodiazepines mostly. Drugs used for sedation. Morphine, pethidine, diazepam, midazolam and the like.'

'Could any of those have been used on Chee?'

Maisie opened her hands to indicate that she didn't know.

Darling stood up. 'Thank you for your help, Maisie.' He extended his hand for her to shake. 'Would you mind if I contacted you again if I have further questions?'

'Not at all,' she said as she walked them to the door.

Darling turned to go and then stopped. 'There is one further thing.' He reached into his jacket pocket and pulled out the plastic bag with the ampoule stump. 'Do you know what this would have contained?'

Maisie looked closely at the yellow band then shook her head. 'But it shouldn't be too hard to find out. Can I keep this? It will take a day or so.'

'I'd appreciate it. It might be nothing,' Darling glanced at Walker, 'but we need to check everything.'

'What do you think about her?' asked Walker after they had left.

Darling walked for some distance along the dark corridor before he answered. 'I think she's telling us all she knows.'

Walker looked at him out of the corner of his eye. 'You know that's not what I meant.'

One wall of the corridor became floor-to-ceiling windows and Darling glanced through them onto a tropical-style garden with soft tree ferns and climbing vines covered in purple flowers. 'Nice,' he said. 'Nice display.'

Walker knew the detective was not talking about the plants.

# CHAPTER TWELVE

PROFESSOR DENIS MCBRENT was a short, red-haired, ruddy-faced man with an equally short temper, and was the head of medicine at the hospital, rarely seen in the clinical areas. So Walker was mildly surprised when he noticed him coming towards him along the cancer centre corridor with his characteristic short, rapid steps.

'Walker,' he barked, raising his hands to bar his progress. 'I need to speak to your registrar, Angela Chee.'

Strangely, Walker thought he seemed agitated, not in his usual curt, aggressive sense, but in a nervous sort of way.

'She'll be here in a moment. We have a clinic this afternoon.'

'Good, I'll wait for her.'

'Is there anything I can help you with? Is it about a patient?' Walker was fairly sure it wouldn't be a clinical question but he figured he may as well sound as if he was trying to be helpful.

'No,' McBrent said brusquely. His face looked like a firecracker ready to explode, but that didn't tell Walker anything. He always looked like that. 'It's about her father.'

'Oh, I see. Terrible thing.'

'How is she standing up to it?'

'Fairly well, actually.'

Walker was surprised McBrent had come out of his way to check on the young doctor. He didn't usually show much consideration for the staff's personal and domestic life. For him, it was all about academic achievement and making his department look good in the eyes of the university. Anything else, including having a dead relative, seemed inconsequential and hardly worth a comment. McBrent had a reputation for not caring two hoots about anyone's feelings, often causing junior staff to burst into tears or worse with his thoughtless, off-hand comments. There had been an investigation a few years ago when one of the interns had committed suicide after a particularly bad roasting from McBrent about the young doctor's lack of clinical acumen. In the end, the university council had concluded that the intern probably suffered from depression and the professor's basting, although poorly timed, was not the direct cause of his suicide. But Walker still had his doubts, so decided he would stay around when McBrent spoke to Angela.

'I thought I had better come and see how you were getting on, Dr Chee,' said McBrent when she turned up for the clinic.

Angela looked appropriately surprised. 'Fine, thank you,' she said warily.

He dropped his voice and put his hand on her shoulder, bowing his head to hers. 'I wonder if I can have a word with you.'

He glanced meaningfully at Walker, who put on a vague expression and raised his eyebrows but stayed put. Walker could see McBrent was irritated but he continued.

'Your father and I were writing a paper together on the effects of diabetes in patients with rheumatoid arthritis. The paper was almost finished and he was updating the references.'

'Yes?' Walker could tell Angela was confused as to why the professor was telling her this.

'Well, the final draft must be at his house, perhaps in his home office. We've searched his office here and it's not there.'

'Yes?' repeated Angela.

'Well, I was wondering if I could come to his house and have a look through his things.' He put on a forced smile. 'It would be a shame for the paper not to be published. He would have wanted it. It would be like his last gift to the literature. Very significant. It was an excellent paper.'

It was the first time since her father's death that Walker saw Angela distressed. 'But I didn't live with my father.'

'But you must have a key?' McBrent insisted.

'Yes, I do.' She looked at Walker, her face twisted in anguish. 'But I'm not sure I want to go there.'

McBrent stiffened. Walker saw his grasp tighten on Angela's shoulder. 'It is very important. He would have wanted it.'

'But ...'

Walker stepped close to her and lifted McBrent's arm off her shoulder. 'Now, Professor McBrent, we don't want to be upsetting Angela, do we?' He clasped his arm around her waist and pulled her away, putting himself between the two of them. He leaned his head close to her ear. 'If you want, I could go with you. I don't think the professor will let up.'

She nodded. There were tears in her eyes. 'Yes, that would be nice. Thank you.'

It was the first time he'd seen her in a fragile state and he felt like hugging her. He resisted. 'No problem. You're my registrar. I have to look after you.' He thought his words might be construed as patronising but it was all he could manage. Either that or lean forward and kiss her.

Walker turned back to McBrent. 'We'll both go.'

For a moment, it looked as if McBrent would explode, his face suffused and his fists curled. But he controlled himself and managed to twist his mouth into the resemblance of a smile. 'Very good, Walker. As soon as possible then. Tonight would be best,' he said quickly, leaving no room for discussion.

Walker considered that he had poked the bear enough so he agreed. 'Tonight then. We'll meet outside Professor Chee's place at six.'

The sun was a glaring red-orange ball on the western horizon and the heat, if anything, was worse than it had been earlier in the day. Walker would have loved to have been sitting at the bar of the Hero of Waterloo sipping on a cold one, or better still, having a bodysurf at Tamarama Beach, but instead, he pulled up right on six outside of Professor Chee's house, a dark-brick Californian bungalow in Epping. On top of the hill opposite rose the tall antenna for Channel Seven, one of Sydney's television stations.

He parked behind a Toyota Landcruiser and could see McBrent's eyes squinting at him through his rear-view mirror. They both remained in their cars, staring at each other without acknowledging the other's presence. Walker felt like he should wave but he didn't like McBrent and waving was for friends. He left his window down since his air conditioning didn't work and the heat was stifling. He wondered idly whether Angela would show.

A few minutes later, she pulled up behind him in a red Honda Prelude, a sporty coupe with flip-up headlights. Walker laughed to himself. 'Just what I thought you'd drive,' he murmured as he got out of the car.

Madonna boomed sexily from oversized speakers while Angela fiddled with the contents of her handbag on her passenger seat, her head down.

Angela cut Madonna off with a twist of her car key and raised her eyes apprehensively to Walker's.

She walked up the path and opened the front door and stood aside to let McBrent and Walker into a small foyer, which led into the lounge room. Straight ahead an open door revealed a bedroom. Angela proceeded to the next door along, Chee's study.

'If you don't mind, I'll have a look through myself,' said McBrent, again wearing an uncharacteristic smile. 'It'll be faster. I know what I'm looking for.'

Walker couldn't remember McBrent ever showing as much as a smirk but today he'd virtually showered both Angela and him with bogus smiles. He didn't like it.

'Of course,' said Angela, looking relieved. 'We'll sit here in the lounge room.'

Walker and Angela sat at right angles to each other on Edwardian armchairs. Walker imagined that her parents used them, at least when her mother had been alive. He wondered how long Angela had been alone with her father. She made a point of taking the green chair, leaving the red winged chair to him. Walker had the feeling it had been her father's. She sat meekly with her hands clasped on her knees while McBrent rummaged around in the office. Walker could hear him flicking through papers, clicking open folders, and opening and closing drawers.

'So, you didn't live with your father?' Walker ventured after a while.

Angela didn't look at him but instead seemed to focus on a spot in the carpet, her forehead wrinkled with anxiety, biting her bottom lip. But she must have heard him since she shook her head. Walker gave up and let his eyes wander around the room. On top of an antique display cabinet with a curved glass front, full of patterned plates and Lladro figurines, were several framed photographs, and Walker went to examine them. There was one of Angela as a teenager in a private girls' school uniform, wearing braces and her hair in plaits. Another was a black and white of three Asian men dressed in army fatigues standing together looking solemnly at the camera. They seemed to be in a jungle and two of them held rifles. The third man looked like a much younger version of Professor Chee.

The last photo was presumably of Chee and his wife on their wedding day. The woman was unmistakably Angela's mother – very beautiful with high cheekbones, full lips and a bright smile. Even accounting for the fact that Asian men held their looks as they got older, he could see the age difference was significant. Angela's mother looked like a teenager, whereas Chee would have had to be in his thirties, by Walker's reckoning.

There was a loud thump of a desk drawer closed roughly and McBrent came out of the office. 'I can't find it.'

'Maybe it's in his office at work?' suggested Walker.

'I told you, it's not there. I've already looked.'

'Must be some paper for you to go to so much trouble.'

For a moment, Walker thought McBrent would burst with anger, sucking in a chest full of air. But again, the red-haired professor visibly calmed himself, taking a few deep breaths as he opened and closed his fists.

'As I said,' he replied in a tight, low voice, 'we've put a lot of work into this paper.' Again, he forced a smile and turned to Angela. 'I would hate to see all your father's work go to waste.' He pointed into the office. 'Angela, there's a locked filing cabinet there. Do you have the key? I feel sure it must be in there.'

She shook her head. 'I have no idea where he kept it. I haven't lived here since my mother died.'

McBrent let out a frustrated breath. 'Can we break it open then? There must be many important papers in there. You'll need to do it sooner or later.'

'I'd rather you didn't.'

'How will you open it then?'

'I'll find the key eventually.' She waved her hand around the house. 'I'll need to go through all this stuff.'

McBrent continued in a barely controlled voice. 'But it may be too late. Someone else will publish.'

Angela's face was blank as she struggled to control her emotions.

Walker intervened. 'I think that will be all for tonight, Professor McBrent.'

'No one asked you, Walker,' he snapped, no longer able to contain his anger. 'This has nothing to do with you.' His face twisted with rage and he stepped towards the younger doctor.

McBrent's attitude would have intimidated most other doctors, many of whom had grown up in privileged environments. But Walker hadn't. He'd seen his first dead body when he was six – a drug murder in one of the backstreets – and had been in more street fights than he could remember. He'd only finally stopped carrying a flick-knife in second year of medical school when it dawned on him that most normal people outside of his neighbourhood didn't have one.

Walker crossed his hands calmly in front and moved a step closer to the older doctor. He spoke in a soft voice. 'I said that will be all for tonight, professor.' He held McBrent's glare. 'Would you like some help getting into your car, sir?'

At first, it looked like McBrent would lash out. He gritted his teeth like an animal and slowly raised his fist. But Walker's calm stare made him hesitate.

'Bah! Fuck you, Walker.' He moved towards the door but turned before he went through. 'Watch yourself, Walker. You don't want me as an enemy, I can promise you that.'

Angela watched him go, wide-eyed and visibly shaken. 'What would you have done if he'd punched you?'

Walker screwed up his face. 'Punch him back, probably. And hope to hell I didn't kill him, I suppose.'

'Kill him? Have you killed someone?'

He shook his head. 'Not in a fight. But I've come close.'

'Not in a fight,' she murmured. She didn't ask the obvious follow-on question.

'Anyway,' said Walker, keen to change the subject. 'What about the key to the cabinet. Shall we look for it?'

Angela slumped back into the chair, looking exhausted. 'I suppose so. I don't want to come back here again any time soon.'

'Where do think it's most likely to be?'

At first, Angela didn't seem to have heard him, having gone back to blankly staring at the spot on the carpet. But then she roused. 'His bedroom probably.' Her voice was laced with dread.

'Shall we look then?'

Again, it seemed as if she hadn't heard, but finally she nodded and walked stiffly towards the door. She paused as if gathering strength before pushing it open. She remained standing in the doorway staring dumbly ahead.

'We don't have to do this, Angela.'

'It's okay,' she said numbly. 'Thank you for helping me.'

Walker shrugged uncomfortably. 'No problem,' he mumbled, unnerved by her distracted reaction.

She stepped into the room and he followed gingerly. But it was just a normal bedroom with a double bed in the middle and a satin bedhead hard up against the opposite wall. Above it was a picture of a pair of black and white storks posing in a bamboo field, their legs intertwined. The bedspread was maroon with a stylised dragon embroidered in silver. There were windows to the right and alongside the opposite wall was a large dark-timbered antique wardrobe.

Angela stood for some time staring into the room, breathing deeply. Finally, she moved towards the nearest bedside cabinet: black Art Deco with a gold Chinese-design inlay. The drawer and cupboard below were empty. She looked up at Walker. 'My mother's.'

She took a deep breath and moved to the other side. Her hand hovered over the drawer and then, with what seemed a great effort of will, opened it and stared in. Walker looked over her shoulder. The contents seemed innocuous: a slim book on English grammar, nail clippers and various lotions and lip balms. In the cupboard below was a camera – a Canon SLR. Alongside were several fresh rolls of film.

'Your father took photos as a hobby?'

'Not as a hobby.' She closed the door mechanically. 'It won't be in there.'

On the top of the cabinet was another framed colour photograph of Angela's mother, smiling brightly. Again, Walker was struck by her beauty and her likeness to Angela. This was a more recent photo, probably from the early 1980s according to the clothing style, but she only looked in her early thirties.

'Your mother was very beautiful. What was her name?'

'Lucia. And yes, she was,' Angela said warmly. 'Beautiful on the inside as well as the outside. She was a lovely mother. And a loyal wife.' She said the last as if it was a point to argue over.

Walker had an idea. 'Do you think ...?' He picked up the photo and turned it over. 'Aha!' He showed her the back. There, taped to the backing board, was a key.

In Chee's office, Walker turned the key in the filing cabinet lock while Angela leaned against the desk and looked around the room as if it was unfamiliar. Her anxiety seemed to have eased, and she appeared to have lost interest in the search.

The top drawer contained mostly financial papers: insurance, tax records and the like.

The second and third drawers were filled with scientific papers and Walker spent some time going through them. But they were all old manuscripts, already published; there were no drafts of papers in preparation. The bottom drawer was full of photos. The files at the front contained old black and whites, mostly of Malaysia, Walker guessed, many similar to the photo in the lounge room. Towards the back were several folders individually tied with string. Names were printed in neat handwriting on the binders and Walker recognised many of them – mostly doctors from the hospital. One of them was Denis McBrent.

'This looks like it,' said Walker.

He pulled it out, untied the string and opened the folder. Angela seemed lost in her own world, sitting against the desk with her arms folded looking the other way.

The folder did not contain a draft of a scientific paper but several A4-sized photos. Walker froze when he saw the first. He turned away from Angela and held the folder close.

Initially, he thought it was Angela, naked, in sexual ecstasy. She was on all fours, her breasts brushing the maroon bed cover, mouth open, eyes closed, seemingly in the midst of an orgasm. Or was her face twisted with loathing? He couldn't be sure. The naked figure behind was unmistakable – Denis

McBrent. And then Walker realised it wasn't Angela but her mother. He glanced at her. She hadn't noticed his reaction. Breathing deeply, he turned away and flicked through a few more of the photos, all similar and showing different aspects of McBrent's sexual encounter with Angela's mother, Lucia Chee. The photos were of high quality and obviously taken by a skilled photographer.

Benjamin Chee.

Walker returned the folder and pulled out another and turned away before he opened it. It included another doctor he recognised – a physician who'd died in the mid eighties. He remembered the rumours that he'd been homosexual and had probably died of complications of AIDS. The folder contained photos of a similar sexual liaison with Lucia. Walker was struck by how Angela's mother's recorded sexual climaxes appeared real, at least in the photos. It was hard to know what she was truly thinking – whether she was forced or compliant. He slipped the folder back into place and noted there were at least four other folders – all marked with the names of doctors who held senior positions in the university or hospital.

'Have you got it?' Angela stood behind him, looking over his shoulder.

'No, it wasn't what I thought.' He clasped the folder shut. He didn't think she'd seen.

'What then?'

He turned to face her. 'I think we need to talk.'

'Angela, tell me about your mother. How did she die?'

They were back in the lounge room sitting on the antique chairs.

'My mother? Why? What have you found?' She looked back at her father's office.

'Before we go into that, I'd like to find out more about your mother.'

Angela's face was pale. 'Mum died in 1984. She got a terrible case of pneumonia and died. It came on too quickly. She couldn't be saved.'

'Had she been unwell before that?'

'Perfectly healthy. One night she got sick. I was in first-year medicine. She got a fever and quickly became confused. Father took her to Casualty and the X-rays showed extensive pneumonia in both lungs.' Angela paused, seemingly lost in the past. 'She was dead by the next day. I never got to speak to her.'

'Did they tell you what caused it?'

She shook her head. 'Father sent me to friends. I came back for the funeral.'

Walker decided to change tack. 'Your mother seemed younger than your father.'

'By twenty years. She was only forty-five when she died.'

'Did she have any friends here in Sydney?'

'Not many. She had a friend she used to have coffee with.' She caught his eye. 'A woman, from up the road. Used to work at the TV station – Channel Seven.'

'You couldn't stay with her?'

She shook her head. 'I didn't know her. Never met her. Didn't even know her name.'

'And your father?'

Angela seemed confused. 'What about him?'

'Did he have many friends?'

She slowly shook her head 'I don't think you would call them friends.' Her head seemed to shrink into her shoulders. 'Mostly work colleagues. Doctors from the hospital and academics from the university.'

Walker thought carefully before asking the next question. 'How did you get on with your father after your mother's death?'

'What do you mean?' she said curtly. 'Fine.'

'Did you live with him?'

She turned away and crossed her arms. 'For a time.'

'You moved out?'

She looked back at him. 'Obviously. What has this to do with my mother?'

'Forgive me, Angela, but you didn't seem to be very upset about your father's death. The police are suspicious. It seemed like you didn't get on with him.'

She stared at him, her face full of anguish, and for a moment Walker thought she would open up. But then she stood abruptly and walked towards the front door.

'This is not helping anyone. If you can't find McBrent's papers I suggest we tell him. But frankly, I don't really care if Father's paper is published or not.'

Without looking back, she walked through the front door, and by the time Walker got to the street Angela was pulling away in her Honda. The right blinker flashed a few times and then she was lost to view.


Barry Darling, feet up on his desk and leaning back in his chair, whistled appreciatively and tapped his Italian leather shoes together. He had just opened the first buff-coloured folder that Walker had handed to him.

'Wow, Kit! This is what in the force we call "evidence".' He glanced up. 'If I'm not mistaken, this would be Professor Chee's wife. And unless the dear professor had had some sort of weird plastic surgery,' he pointed a finger at the photo, 'that is not Benjamin Chee.' He flicked through the rest of the photos then opened the next folder. He whistled silently again then quickly examined the contents of the other four folders.

He took his feet off the desk and sat forward. 'How long have you had these? And where did you get them?'

'Yesterday, from Professor Chee's home office.' Walker had been in a quandary about what to do with the files but had decided there was only one answer. As much as it irked him, he realised he had to hand them over to Darling and had called him first thing that morning.

Darling read out the name on the first folder. 'Denis McBrent.' He looked up again. 'Do you know who that is?'

'He's the professor of medicine at the hospital.'

Darling flicked his pencil between his fingers. 'And the others?'

'Other senior doctors with either the hospital or the university. Two have died since, and the other three have retired.'

'Died? What from?'

'That one,' Walker pointed to a folder, 'died of AIDS in the mid eighties. The other I'm not sure. Old age, I guess.'

'AIDS,' Darling said. 'Not the sort of thing heterosexual men usually get. Unless he was a haemophiliac?'

Walker shook his head. 'Not as far as I know.'

'So, we have a bisexual man screwing Chee's wife. And someone taking good-quality photos during the whole session.' He studied the photos again. 'This wasn't someone hiding in a cupboard. Whoever it was was involved in the whole shebang. Got up real close.' He looked up again meaningfully at Walker. 'Chee?'

'Who else?'

Darling continued to flick through the photos. 'And it looks like Mrs Chee was enjoying it. These photos don't strike me as someone having sex under duress.'

'You can't know that just from the photos. She could be hating it.'

He smirked. 'Doesn't look like that to me. Looks like she's having a great old time.'

Walker was unhappy talking about Angela's mother with Darling. But it was more than that, he realised. Somehow, seeing Darling thumbing through them and carefully examining each one made him feel jealous. 'Her name's Lucia,' he blurted.

Darling made a face as if the information was inconsequential. 'Looks a bit like her daughter, don't you think?'

'Not really.'

Darling made a face again and went back to them with an exaggerated, studious look. 'No, I think you're wrong. She looks *very* much like her daughter. Angela, isn't it?'

'Don't you think you've seen enough?' Walker tried to hide the irritation in his voice.

'She *is* very attractive. Looks like a real goer. Looks like she's really enjoying that old fellow pumping into her.'

Walker clamped his jaw tight.

'Like mother, like ...'

Walker stood up abruptly, knocking his chair over. 'I have to get back to the hospital. I've got cancer patients to see.'

Darling was smiling widely. 'Of course, Kit. You get back. I'll take it from here. And thank you very much for showing me these.' He waved one of the photos in the air so Walker could see the naked flesh.

'I didn't show them ...'

Darling's smile widened even further.

Walker turned and lurched out of the room. The corridor was hot and the air stunk of sweating bodies. He needed to get out. He reached the elevators and clicked the down button repeatedly until the door opened. Once outside the building, he breathed in deeply and headed towards the large public park that led back towards the hospital. Slowly, his anger began to settle.

'You're a total tosser, Wendy,' he blurted when he reached a path that wound around the playing fields. A woman walking in the opposite direction gave him a startled look and quickened her pace away from him.

'Sorry!' he called after her, but that only made her walk even faster.

'Always were a total tosser!' he said again, this time with more restraint, as he turned back in the direction of the hospital.

# CHAPTER THIRTEEN

IT WAS TEN thirty in the morning and they finished the departmental meeting early. The two murders had thrown the entire hospital into a spin and the chief administrator had called a meeting of all the heads of department, so the medical oncology meeting had been abandoned.

Walker found Angela waiting in the corridor outside the meeting room with Sandy. It was a hot and humid January day and she was dressed appropriately in an orange shift that stopped at mid-thigh, with her lustrous dark hair pulled up off her neck and held in place with a silver hair comb of Asian design. He thought she might not be wearing a bra, although he couldn't be sure, and he had to force himself not to stare at her chest. Her mother's photos came into his head and he turned away.

'Dr Walker, we have a spare thirty minutes. I think I'll buy you your coffee now.'

Walker was taken unawares. 'Now?' he blurted. He wasn't sure he wanted to be alone with the pretty registrar. If he was seen leaving the hospital with her, he knew the rumour mill, already in full swing with the murders, would go ballistic.

Angela seemed unfazed. 'Yee-Hah will be coming too so you don't have to worry about being seen alone with me.'

Walker feigned surprise. 'Alone with you? What do you mean?'

'Dr Walker, I'm sure you realise I am a suspect in my father's murder and so it's natural that you would feel uncomfortable being with me.'

'Nonsense,' he blustered.

'Nonetheless, I think it would be safer if Yee-Hah came with us.'

'Are you sure he likes coffee?'

'He can have tea if he wishes,' she snapped.

Sandy pushed the glasses back on his nose, seemingly unperturbed by the way they spoke about him as if he wasn't present.

'I want to discharge this wager as quickly as possible,' said Angela. 'I don't like loose ends.'

'Fine then,' he said shortly. 'Let's go and have coffee.'

They took the elevator to the ground floor and made their way through the brightly lit foyer of the hospital, the soaring roof constructed of metal beams arranged to leave triangular spaces covered in perspex which let the sunlight through – welcome in winter but not so appreciated in the height of summer. They weaved their way through the crowd that was perpetually gathered there: patients in hospital gowns pushing IV stands heading outside for a smoke, relatives searching for the ward where their loved one had been admitted, and deliverymen pushing trolleys loaded with goods. Once outside and out of the air conditioning, the heat hit them and Walker moved quickly to the path under the shade of the trees in the small park in front of the hospital entrance.

'Bloody hot!' he exclaimed. 'But I suppose this is nothing to you two.'

Angela smiled but Sandy didn't look happy. 'I do not enjoy this heat,' he stated in his staccato way. 'In KL, buildings are all air conditioned and we don't walk outside like this.' He frowned. 'Only coolies and office workers on lunch break walk on street in heat of day, *lah*.'

'Come on, Yee-Hah, it's not *that* hot,' said Angela.

'You *siao ah*, Angela! This is just as hot as Singapore.'

Angela rolled her eyes. *'Walao, eh! Kai pei la!'*

'Okay, okay. *Paiseh ah*. Maybe not as hot.' He frowned up at the sun. 'I will be okay.'

'Very good,' she said sarcastically. 'Come, I clap for you.'

'Okay, okay. But at least you *belanja* me.'

'I said I would. Stop complaining, Yee-Hah, you're such a baby.'

Walker listened to the conversation, smiling, as they climbed the slight rise to the main road. He also noticed how Angela seamlessly slipped from English into Singlish, including a change of accent, as if they were two completely different languages. For some reason it made her seem even more attractive.

They scurried across the road – the soaring temperature compounded by the radiant heat from the black asphalt – and reached an old Federation cottage that had been converted into a cafe. The place had no air conditioning and the large ceiling fans seemed to have little effect on the stifling heat. The room was mostly empty with only a few tables taken by nurses on their break, and a teenage girl who was probably wagging school.

Angela addressed the plump lady with a thick head of grey hair who smiled at them from behind the counter. 'Cappuccino for me, please.' She turned to her guests. 'And you, Dr Walker?'

'Coke, thanks, with ice in a glass.'

'Yee-Hah?'

'*Cincai lah.*' Sandy flapped his hands indolently, looking very unhappy with the heat. 'Anything *lor*, whatever *lor*.'

'Coffee?'

Sandy shook his head. 'Don't want.'

'Tea then?'

'Don't want.'

'Then what?'

'I said *cincai lah*! Whatever you think.'

'You will have tea then.'

Sandy raised his palms and took a seat at one of the small tables under a large ceiling fan.

They sat in silence while they waited for their orders to arrive. Sandy waved a doubled-over piece of paper before his face, blowing out air every few moments as if he might keel over at any time while Angela tutted and shook her head at his antics.

'Does your home have air conditioning in KL, Sandy?' asked Walker

'Now, yes. But before, no. My family is not very rich.'

'What do they do?'

'My father works in a factory and my mother is a sales assistant in Jaya Jusco department store. They worked very hard to save money for me to go to university.' Walker thought Sandy looked embarrassed. 'But my family were not always so lowly. My grandfather used to work for the British back in the fifties until ...' He paused in thought.

'Until?' prompted Angela.

'Until he didn't work for them anymore.' He picked up the menu that sat on the table. 'Maybe I should have had a Coke.'

'Too late now, Yee-Hah,' Angela said bossily. 'Next time be more assertive. Now you will get what I say.'

Sandy stuck out his lip and continued to stare at the menu. Angela looked out of the window and Walker followed her gaze. The sky was an unbroken blue strip above the squat concrete walls of the hospital, which began across the road and down a slope. From here they could see the top of the thick plain walls of the radiotherapy bunkers and above them, the rest of the hospital – three long, fortress-like solid blocks, set one behind the other. Viewed from the outside, Walker conceded that it really was quite an ugly building. It had been erected in a hurry in the late seventies as part of the then prime minister Gough Whitlam's plan to expand health care to the burgeoning outer suburbs of Sydney. Only a dozen years later its brutalist architecture already appeared outdated.

Finally, their drinks arrived and Walker took a large swig of his Coke while Angela sipped on her cappuccino. It was clear that Walker would have to maintain the conversation so he cleared his throat.

'Angela, I should ask you again whether you are coping with work. With your father and everything.'

'Of course.' She played with the froth of her coffee and it became clear she wasn't about to elucidate.

'What about the funeral then? You'll need to have time off. When is it?'

'Detective Darling hasn't yet told me when the body will be released.'

Again, Walker was struck by her indifference. 'Do you have family who can help?'

She shook her head. 'No family. All back in Malaysia. I don't really know them. None are close. A few cousins.'

'Malaysia? I thought you were from Singapore.'

'I am. My father was from Malaysia. And all his family, or what's left of it.'

'What about your mother's side? Are they coming?'

'They were not close to my father.' Her tone was short. 'They would not be interested.'

'But what about you? Wouldn't they want to come to be with you?'

Now Walker recognised true sadness in her eyes as she shook her head. 'They would not be interested,' she repeated. 'I don't really know them. They didn't want my mother to marry my father and so I've never met them.' She gave Walker an uncomfortable look, as if she'd said more than she intended.

'That's very sad,' he said and he meant it. He resisted the temptation to reach for her hand. She looked into his eyes and, for a change, he saw true emotion. Her eyes were brown and soft and threatened tears. He wanted to touch her cheek. He placed his hand on the table near hers. She looked down at it but did not move hers.

'This tea is too hot.' Sandy banged the cup back down on the table and some liquid splashed onto the surface. 'And it's got perfume in it. It's not proper tea.'

'*Eeyer*, it's Earl Grey, *goondu*,' said Angela. She seemed grateful for the interruption. 'Next time I give you *kopi-C*.'

'No *kopi-C. Kopi Gau*. I have real coffee.'

She flapped her hands. 'Whatever, *lah*.' Despite her words, Angela seemed pleased and Walker guessed she found some comfort in speaking the language of her childhood.

He gulped down the rest of his Coke. 'That's it then. I have to get back. Thanks for the drink, Angela. You can now consider our wager settled.' He decided to be flippant to match their conversation. 'But more importantly, you have learned an important lesson about respecting your superior's knowledge. Next time you'll think twice.'

But instead of getting a laugh from her, she bowed her head demurely. 'Thank you, Dr Walker. You are correct. I will try to give you the proper respect you deserve in future.'

He wondered whether she was being sarcastic but then, with some embarrassment, he realised she was serious. 'Angela, I was only joking.'

'No,' she answered, 'I promise I will be diligent in learning as much as I can from you from now on.'

Walker let out a breath through puffed cheeks. 'Okay then.'

'And I have not met the wager.' Now her brown eyes were raised towards his from her bowed head. 'I was to buy you a coffee, not a Coke. I will have to take you out again.'

Walker crinkled his mouth hesitantly. 'Okay,' he said slowly. He couldn't be sure but he thought he could see the beginnings of a smile on the corner of her lips.


When they returned to the hospital, Detective Darling was waiting for them in the ward.

'Have time to go out for coffee with your young registrar, do you, Kit? I thought you said you needed to get away for your patients?'

'What do you want, Wendy?'

'I need to speak to Dr Chee.'

The detective took her aside, making it clear that Walker was not to be involved. Walker stood with Sandy watching them talk in the empty corridor further away, trying to discern what Darling was saying.

'They're really picking on poor Dr Chee,' said a voice nearby and Walker turned to see Andy Korbmann standing with Gloria. 'Her father was a nasty piece of work but his daughter is definitely *not* like him.'

'I didn't know you knew Professor Chee,' said Walker.

'I didn't really,' said Andy. 'I helped him with something a few years ago. But the professor's character led him to fail his degrees.'

'What does that mean?' asked Sandy. 'Why would a professor do another degree?'

Andy rubbed his mouth roughly. 'Nothing. I didn't mean that.' He pointed along the corridor to where Darling was interrogating Angela. 'What I meant to say is that the police should leave her alone. She had nothing to do with it. They should get on with their job and find the killer.'

Walker thought he knew what Andy was talking about and was about to clarify with him when he was interrupted by Angela returning. Darling was walking away in the opposite direction. 'He wants to search my father's house,' said Angela. 'This afternoon, with me there. He has a warrant.'

Walker had been expecting that. 'Do you want me to be there?'

'Would you?' Her brown eyes looked grateful.

'Of course. What time shall I meet you there?'


Detective Darling met Angela at her father's house that evening after she had finished work. When she pulled up, he was already waiting in his white Commodore, parked under the shade of one of the brush-boxes that lined the street. Across the road was a marked police car with Constable Jones at the wheel and a female officer in the passenger seat. Darling got out of his car and stood on the footpath while Angela fiddled with her bag, her engine still idling. Finally, she switched it off and got out of the car, twisting her long

## Murder on the Ward

lean legs onto the road and pulling down her tight skirt as she stood up. She looked up and down the street, then let out a deep breath.

'Expecting someone?' asked Darling.

'Dr Walker said he would come to be with me. I shouldn't really have asked him.' She paused and looked at her father's house. 'But I really don't like coming here.'

'And why is that, Angela?' Darling's voice was gentle, nothing like the brashness he normally displayed, especially when he was around Walker. 'What did you have against your father? It's obvious that you weren't close. It would help me understand the situation if you could tell me a bit about your relationship with him.'

Angela moved to stand under the shade of the tree, her head bowed, her dark hair hanging gracefully to partially obscure her face. Then she pulled the hair back with one hand, her face defiant. 'I'd rather not say.'

'It will come out eventually.'

'Why? It has nothing to do with my father's death.'

'I wish I could believe that. But I have a very strong impression that your relationship with your father has everything to do with his murder.'

Her face was stiff. 'I had nothing to do with my father's death.'

'Yes. And that includes nothing to do with his attempted resuscitation.'

'I knew he was dead. Resuscitation was futile.'

'Angela, that's not good enough. You guys are trained to resuscitate. It's an instinct. Something stopped you, and not just because you *thought* it was futile. You either *knew* he was already dead. Or you hated him so much you wanted him dead.'

She said nothing to that and bowed her head again then looked up as Walker pulled up behind Angela's car. He quickly joined them.

'Sorry I'm late.'

'No matter,' said Darling. 'It gave Angela and I time to have a little talk.'

Walker frowned at Darling and then at her.

'Let's get this over with,' she said.

Angela and Walker stood together in silence in the lounge room as Darling, Constable Jones and the female officer searched first Chee's office and then the bedroom. Angela, her arms crossed tightly across her chest, stared at the camera in Jones's hand when they finally came out.

'Where's your mother's stuff?' asked Darling.

'She's been gone for over five years. Father must have got rid of it all.'

'He didn't give you anything? Any jewellery?'

Angela's lips tightened and she gave a single shake of her head.

Darling went to the display cabinet in the lounge room. 'Who's this?' he asked, pointing to the photo of the three men in army fatigues.

'One is my father,' said Angela. 'I don't know who the other two are.'

'Where was it taken?'

Angela lifted her hands 'Before I was born. Malaysia, I guess.'

'You never asked your father?'

'No.'

Darling raised his brow. 'Was he in the army?'

'Looks like it,' she said tightly. 'Unless he was at a fancy-dress party.'

Darling stared at her intently then slowly smiled. 'Good one, Angela. You're making jokes. I'd call that progress.' He lifted the photo. 'Do you mind if we take this?'

'Not at all.'

'We may as well take all three,' he said, pointing to the other two photos: Angela as a schoolgirl and the other of her mother on her wedding day. He gestured to the female officer who placed them all into a bag that Jones held open.

'What do you need the other two for?' barked Walker.

'What's it to you?' Darling returned calmly. He looked from Angela back to Walker, his eyebrows raised.

Walker flicked his eyes to Angela then looked away. 'Nothing, I suppose.'

'Okay with you, Angela?'

'I will want my mother's picture when you have finished with it.'

'Of course you will,' Darling agreed. 'And the photo of your father?'

She said nothing.

'Show me the rest of the house,' said Darling.

Angela led them through another door into the kitchen and then through to an annex that appeared to have been added to the rear of the house after it was built. There was a bathroom, a laundry and another room at the very back. Angela pointed at the door. 'My old bedroom.'

Walker hung behind, uncertain of what to expect of Angela's old room. Wall posters of boy bands? Pink heart cushions and teddy bears? But when she pushed the door open, it was clear the room hadn't been used in a long while. The wardrobe had its doors ajar and appeared empty except for a pair of Dunlop Volleys and an old string bag sitting in the bottom. He followed Darling and Angela into the room but lingered near the door. On the other wall was a cheap pinewood chest, its drawers half open containing an old Hubba Bubba packet and a bitten-off pencil stub. There was no bed, and no pictures on the buff-coloured walls, just dirty smudges and a thin crack in the plaster running diagonally under the single rear window. The blind looked broken, pulled halfway up on one side. An orange beanbag sat in the corner away from the door, a gap in the top of the zip visible, with a small pile of styrofoam pellets spilled on the floor beside it.

'You didn't come back to stay on the weekends?' Darling asked sarcastically.

'What for?' she answered flatly. 'I have a unit not far from here near the station. I can walk to it.'

Walker felt that the room had a sense of loneliness and sadness. The only evidence left by the previous occupant was a sticker on the wardrobe door that read *The Benny Hill Show* in pink bubble-text with a picture of the actor dressed as a bus conductor, his cap askew and wearing thick black-rimmed glasses. There had been other stickers but those had been torn off leaving thin paper scars on the fake oak veneer.

Darling quickly went through the wardrobe and drawers and, satisfied there was nothing to find, led them back into the lounge room. By that time, Jones and the female officer had bundled the contents of Chee's filing cabinet and desk into cardboard boxes, and these were stacked on hand trolleys ready to go.

'I think that's the lot,' he announced and the team began to wheel them out. Darling motioned for Angela and Walker to follow them.

'Just one last thing, Dr Chee,' he said as Angela reached her car. 'We need you to come down to the station tomorrow. I'd like you to answer a few more questions.'

The sun had set and the flaming orange band on the western horizon reflected on their faces, giving Angela a golden glow. Walker thought it made Darling appear jaundiced.

'Do I have a choice?'

'Of course,' he said, smiling. 'Unless we arrest you. Then you'll have to come.'

Angela frowned and bit her bottom lip in thought. She glanced at Walker before answering. 'Can I bring a lawyer?'

'Yep. I would if I were you.' Darling looked at Walker and then back at Angela. 'But this time leave the doc here at the hospital. No more babysitters. From now on we get real.'

Walker and Angela watched as Darling drove away, the V8 gunning up the street before he took the first right.

'What a dickhead,' Walker huffed. 'Didn't even use his blinker.' He turned back to Angela who leaned against the bonnet of her car, her bare shoulders slumped and her dark hair falling forward over her bowed head. But when she sensed he was looking at her, she lifted her face, pulled her hair back and gave him a smile.

'You look tired,' he said softly.

She gave a noncommittal shrug of her shoulders.

Walker hesitated. 'Do you ... do you want to get a drink?'


Walker and Angela each drove their own cars and parked them in the carpark of a supermarket then crossed to the back entrance of the Epping Hotel. Stairs led downwards to the Tracks nightclub, which was closed at this time of day. The poster next to the door declared that 'Pearl Jammed' would be playing there that Friday night.

'Who are they?' Walker asked. When she didn't answer he added, 'Tribute band for sure.'

They walked up the stairs to the hotel lounge and Angela took a seat at a small table near the wall. 'I'm meeting my lawyer here. It's quieter so we can talk.'

'Your lawyer? When did you have time to call her?'

'Didn't. She's always here on a Thursday night.'

'Oh,' Walker said sombrely. 'So you were coming to the pub anyway?'

'No. I want to catch her before she gets plastered.'

'Plastered?' He gave a short laugh. 'Very funny, Angela. What would you like to drink?'

A few minutes later he was wandering back towards their table carrying a beer for himself and a chardonnay for her, when he caught sight of a woman standing talking to Angela. He slowed down so he could take in the sight. She was tall with brown-blonde hair and a slim, muscular body wrapped in a short clingy dress that revealed long shapely legs. She was talking animatedly with Angela. He stopped behind her uncertainly. The woman sensed his presence when Angela looked at him and she spun around and flashed him a broad smile.

Walker was taken aback by her looks. She *had* to be a model of some sort. His mouth opened and he thought he said something but he wasn't certain what it was.

The woman's smile stretched even further and she let out a playful giggle. 'Wow. Smooth talker.'

'S ...sorry,' he stammered and plonked the drink down, spilling some of it onto his hand and table. He wiped his palm and held it out for her to shake then realised beer was dripping from it. He went to pull his hand back, but she was too fast and grabbed his palm and held it tight. She pulled him closer. Intimately. 'Cassandra Hollow,' she said in a low voice and gave him a questioning smile.

'Chris Walker,' he blurted. 'Pleased to meet you.'

She looked over her shoulder and spoke to Angela. 'Is this your boss? You didn't tell me he was so young.' She looked back at Walker, still clasping his hand. 'And spunky too.' She pulled him a little closer. 'How old are you?'

'Thirty-three,' he said.

She shook his hand slowly. 'Thirty-three and a specialist. Impressive. Angela and I are thirty and look at us.'

Walker looked from Angela back to Cassandra, one dark, the other blonde. The lawyer stepped backwards and stuck a pose as if to give him an opportunity to examine her whole body, pushing out a full chest and placing one long leg forward, a bright smile on full lips.

'Very nice,' he said, breathlessly

'That's enough, Cassie,' Angela said finally, although her voice was kind. 'Must you torture all of my friends like that?'

Cassandra spun around and stepped beside her. 'Don't be silly, Ange, I'm only having a bit of fun. Chris enjoyed it, didn't you, Chris?'

Walker gave a stupid smile, not trusting himself to answer. 'Would you like a drink?'

'VB,' she answered. 'Schooner.'

By the time he got back, the girls had their heads together in serious conversation. Cassandra grabbed the beer when he handed it to her and took a long gulp.

'What time tomorrow?' she said to Angela. 'I'll have to cancel a few things if it's in the morning. What's the name of the detective?'

He gasped. 'You're Angela's lawyer?'

They both turned to him, their faces equally stern. 'Are you sure he's your boss?' Cassandra said to Angela then turned to Walker. 'Yes, I'm her lawyer.' Then she flicked her head to the side. 'Well, we live together and I'm a lawyer, so it only makes sense.'

He took a long swig of his beer and gave a smile. 'Are you a criminal lawyer?'

'Of course I'm a criminal lawyer. Would Angela get someone who does conveyancing to help her with the police?'

'Nope. No, she would not.' His smile widened further. 'Wendy's going to love this.'

'Who's Wendy?'

'The detective,' said Angela.

'I'm confused,' she said turning back to her friend. 'I thought the detective was a man.'

'He is,' said Angela. 'It's Chris's nickname for him. Look, we don't have time to go into that now. I've told you all I know. You go and enjoy yourself. I'll see you later tonight.'

Cassandra gave Angela a kiss and Walker a short wave then began to move away.

'Cassie,' Angela called out, causing her to spin smoothly on long, lean legs. 'I *will* see you tonight, won't I?'

But all Cassandra gave her was a wide smile and another wave before she wandered off into the crowd.

They met at nine the next morning outside the Parramatta police station, a utilitarian three-storey brown block that sat next to a courthouse of similar construction. Walker had arrived early after receiving a call from Angela that morning asking him to come with her, claiming that Cassandra said she needed to bring a friend. Walker pondered why Angela had chosen him. Didn't she have other friends? He also wondered how she had his home number.

Cassandra and Angela turned up separately even though they lived together, and Walker wondered whether the tall blonde had made it home the night before, after all.

Cassandra called out before she reached him. 'I have to race off after this and Angela insists she's going back to the hospital afterwards, so she drove herself.'

Angela reached them from the opposite direction, coming from the large park that sat between the Parramatta shops and the hospital.

'Are you sure it's all right me coming?' asked Walker. 'Detective Darling was insistent that I didn't.'

Cassandra huffed. 'Typical copper! Try to get away with anything. Angela has the right to legal representation,' she tapped her chest, 'and to have a friend or relative present at the interview.' She pointed to Walker. 'Don't worry. If this ... Wendy – or whatever his name is – causes trouble, I'll sort him out.'

They entered together and were signed in at the front desk by the same cheerful, plump clerk who then led them to the second floor. Darling greeted them in the corridor, giving Walker a brief frown before turning his attention to the leggy beauty who confidently offered her hand for him to shake. She wore a white blouse discreetly open at the front and a black skirt split on one leg.

'Cassandra Hollow, criminal lawyer at Huntley and Miers, representing Angela Chee. I've asked Dr Walker to attend to give Angela support.'

Walker was struck by her change in manner. Last night in the pub, she had been – well, a bit slutty. Now she was a polished professional.

'Detective Sergeant Barry Darling. Pleased to meet you, Ms Hollow.' He smiled broadly, still holding her hand as his eyes flashed from her face down and up her body and back to her brown eyes. 'I don't think we need worry Dr Walker here. I'm sure he has work to do back at the hospital.' He looked meaningfully at Walker. 'Don't you, Kit?'

Cassandra smiled back calmly. 'Dr Walker will be joining us,' she said firmly 'Where will we speak?'

Darling frowned but said no more as he led them to a small room with a single window and a plain desk and chairs.

'You sit there, Kit,' he said, stabbing a finger at a chair in the corner as he took his seat at the table on the side closest to the door. The women sat on the other side, Angela biting the inside of her lip, her face pale. Cassandra crossed her legs and clasped her knee with intertwined hands.

Soon after Constable Jones joined them and Darling introduced him. 'Shall we start?'

Cassandra opened her hands in affirmation.

'This interview is in relation to the death of Professor Benjamin Chee. Angela, we want to ask you some questions about it but, under law, we are not allowed to ask you these questions without giving you your cautions and your rights. Do you understand that?'

Angela shot Cassandra a nervous look then turned back to Darling.

'Am I under arrest?'

'No.'

'What are my rights?

'I'll give you the rights straight up just so that we're perfectly clear,' said Darling. 'The first one is that you do have the right to remain silent. That means that you do not have to say anything, answer any questions or give any statements unless you wish to do so. We are recording our conversation and that may later be used in evidence in court if we ever get that far. Do you understand that?'

Angela nodded.

'You will need to assent verbally for the record,' said Jones.

'Yes, go ahead,' said Angela stiffly.

'I have to ask you some standard questions. Can I ask how old you are?'

'I'm thirty years of age.'

'And are you a person of Aboriginal or Torres Strait Islander heritage?'

'Does it really matter?'

'No. Well, it doesn't really matter but it's something that we're required to ask.'

'Okay, no.'

'Are you a foreign national?'

'I'm Australian.'

'Australian. You don't hold citizenship in any other country?'

'I was born in Singapore but I'm an Australian citizen.'

'And are you under the influence of a drug or alcohol at present?'

'No. Maybe last night.'

'Maybe last night?'

'Alcohol only.'

'Okay. That's all the legal stuff I have to ask you.' Darling slouched back in his chair. 'Angela, you understand that we believe your father was murdered – given an overdose of a drug that stopped his heart.' He glanced down at his notepad. 'Metoprolol.'

'Yes.'

'First, we want to ask you about the circumstances surrounding his death and your reaction to it. You and Dr Walker here, first saw your father in his hospital room, is that correct?'

'Yes.'

'What was his condition when you saw him?'

'He was dead.'

'Dead? How did you ascertain that?'

'I could see.'

'Did you feel for a pulse, check that he was breathing? That sort of thing?'

Angela spoke through tight lips. 'I checked his pulse. As I said, he was already gone.'

'But Dr Walker called an arrest. He's had more experience than you. How is it that you could tell your father was dead but Dr Walker thought he could be resuscitated?'

'You just said it,' Cassandra interjected. 'Dr Walker has more experience. He could make a better assessment. Are you blaming Dr Chee for being inexperienced?'

'But don't you see, *she* made the better assessment,' Darling countered. 'He wasn't able to be resuscitated by an experienced team. Dr Walker was wrong. Dr Chee was right. The question is – how could she know it was futile?'

'That is pure supposition, Detective Darling,' Cassandra said firmly. She made a motion as if to stand. 'If this is the only evidence you have, you're wasting our time.'

Darling waved a hand for her to remain seated. 'The point I'm making is that Dr Chee seemed too sure that her father was dead. As if she already knew. Not that he couldn't be resuscitated. No, she *knew* he was dead.'

'That's a bit far-fetched,"' Cassandra replied.

'She didn't say that her father could not be resuscitated. That could be put down to inexperience. She was sure he was dead. There's a difference.'

'I think you're reading too much into it, Detective Darling. Angela was in shock.'

'As everyone keeps saying,' he said dryly. 'A doctor who has taken part in many resuscitations, in shock? I don't buy it. Forgive me, but if I found my father unconscious, I would try to save him, especially if I were a trained doctor.'

Walker had to stop from interjecting You don't even know who your father is.

Cassandra let out an exasperated breath. 'Again, if all you have is your *feelings* and no evidence –'

Darling interrupted her by raising a hand and fixed Angela with a stare. 'I'll ask again. How did you know your father was dead?'

'I could just tell.' Her voice was tight.

'You could just tell. So, when Dr Walker had determined that your father was ... what? In need of the arrest team, what did you do?'

She shook her head. 'Nothing.'

'Nothing?'

'As I said, I could see he was dead.'

Darling paused and examined Angela carefully before speaking again. 'Did you help with the resuscitation?'

'No.'

'How did it go then?'

'Dr Walker started chest compression and then the arrest team arrived and took over.'

'Did you give mouth-to-mouth while you waited? The more experienced physician had deemed it possible to resuscitate him. He thought that your father could be saved. But you didn't feel impelled to help? To save your own father?'

'No.'

'Why not? It must have been a few minutes before they arrived.'

'I already told you.'

'You knew he was dead.'

Cassandra interrupted. 'That is not what Angela said, Detective Darling. She said she could *see* he was dead.'

Darling paused then glanced down at his pad before speaking. 'Angela, I'll ask you again, did you *know* your father was dead?'

'Angela, you don't have to answer that,' said Cassandra.

Angela sat looking straight forward, her eyes unfocused, her face emotionless. Darling spent some moments watching her before continuing.

'Angela, were you upset about your father's death?'

'Of course.' Her voice was mechanical.

'Forgive me, but from the statements made, you didn't seem very upset.'

Cassandra interrupted. 'People respond to shock in different ways.'

'There's that defence again. Shock.' Darling shook his head dismissively and glanced down at his pad. '"Shell-shocked" was the word used. In fact, you wanted to keep working, didn't you? You wanted to finish the round with Dr Walker but you were sent home against your will. And you didn't take any time off work. You turned up the next day, bright and early. That doesn't sound as if you were upset. It couldn't have been shellshock the next day.'

Walker remembered Angela's reaction at the time. No one has a father like mine, she said. I can assure you, he will not be missed.

Cassandra interrupted again. 'I'll repeat myself, everyone reacts differently to stress, Detective Darling. Some continue to work. They like to do what is familiar.'

'That's true, but we have had a number of witnesses who were struck by how unusually calm Angela was at the time. More than one witness.'

Cassandra stood. 'I think we can say we are finished, Detective Darling. You have had ample time to provide evidence but all you have given is your opinion. Angela, we can leave now.'

Darling interjected. 'Angela, what was your relationship with your father like before he died?'

She froze in the act of rising. 'Relationship?'

'Yes. Did you see each other a lot, have dinner? That sort of thing.'

'Not much.' She sat back in her seat.

'But you only lived around the corner. When was the last time you met with him?'

'I can't remember.'

'Try. You don't have to give me dates or anything, just approximately.'

'I don't know, maybe a year?'

'A year! And what was that for?'

'I went to his place to ask for some of Mum's things.'

'And did he give them to you?'

'No.' She looked down at the table. 'He'd thrown everything out.'

'Must have made you angry?'

'Not really. I expected it. It was the sort of thing he would do.'

'You didn't like your father much, did you?'

She continued to look down. 'Not much.'

Darling paused meaningfully. 'Why is that?'

'You don't have to answer that,' said Cassandra, still standing.

'He wasn't good to my mother.'

'In what way?'

'He made her do things that were not nice.'

'Things?'

Angela looked straight at Darling for the first time. 'You *know*. You have the photos. They were in the boxes that you took.'

'Made her have sex with other men?' persisted Darling.

'Yes.'

'Is that all?'

'Isn't that enough?'

'Did he do anything to you?'

Angela froze, her face wooden. She shook her head once.

'Did he do the same?'

'I don't want to talk about it.' Her voice was numb.

'Did he make you have sex with other men? Did he have sex with you?'

Cassandra Hollow's commanding voice cut into the room. 'She said she doesn't want to talk about it, Detective Darling.' She put her hand on Angela's wrist. 'Don't say anything more. I think that will be all, detective. Close off your interview.'

Darling looked down out of the second-floor window at the trio who had gathered outside the entrance of the police building. Cassandra Hollow was speaking energetically to

Angela Chee, who merely nodded, stony-faced, while Walker listened.

He realised he hadn't handled the last part of the interview well, but overall, he was pleased. He had put Chee's daughter on notice. Maybe she would make a mistake?

From his position, hidden by the edge of the window, he could study the lawyer's profile and he examined her from top to bottom, her full blonde hair, slender neck, long legs.

He let out a low whistle.

'Back to work, Barry,' he murmured to himself as he turned away.

He held a stack of folders that contained the photos of Angela's mother's sexual liaisons in his palm as if he were trying to guess their weight, then threw them onto the desk.

He looked at his wristwatch then pulled the notepad from his pocket and flicked through the pages before stopping at one. He picked up the phone and punched in a number.

'This is Detective Barry Darling from the New South Wales Police Service in Sydney. Your International Cooperation Department suggested I call you. They said they would let you know.'

A female voice replied, 'Thank you for calling, detective. May I ask what it is about?'

'Yes, it's about a murder case we're investigating here in Sydney.'

'Who would you like to speak to?'

'The deputy director, please. Criminal Investigation.'

While he waited to be put through, he opened another folder and stared down at the contents – the photo of Benjamin Chee in army fatigues in a tropical jungle with two other figures. He picked up the photo and stepped from foot to foot restlessly as he looked out the window.

'This is Director Hung Tan.' The voice was deep with hardly an accent. 'How can I help you?'

Darling frowned. 'Director Hung Tan. Sorry, I was expecting the Deputy Director.'

'Is that Detective Barry Darling?'

'Yes, sir. From Parramatta in Sydney.'

'We got your fax. I thought I had better take your call.'

Darling flicked the photo in his hand. 'Thank you, sir. As I mentioned in the fax, I was hoping you could help us with a case. A murder. The victim was a Singaporean.'

'Go on.'

He threw the photo back on his desk, his nervousness gone. 'We would like you to identify two men in a photograph.'

'We can try.'

'That would be much appreciated.' Darling paused before continuing. 'I think it was taken during the Malayan Emergency.'

## CHAPTER FOURTEEN

THAT EVENING, CHRISTOPHER Walker walked through the front door of the Captain Cook, a local pub near the corner of Kent and Argyle streets, up the road from where he lived. The pub was one of the few in The Rocks district that was not on the tourist path, mostly frequented by the local housing commission tenants, wharfies, tradesmen and the Friday night office crowds. It was a real pub, a good, honest watering hole with no fancy boutique beers or food and, in Walker's opinion, was what a local pub was supposed to be for – drinking and talking. And in the case of the Captain Cook, making deals.

Walker was there to meet an old friend and he found him seated at the bar, nursing a schooner in a meaty hand. He had the appearance of an unsuccessful businessman – overweight, balding, ruddy-faced and wearing a shabby suit – but Walker knew for a fact that Bruce Rowntree was loaded, having garnered a significant fortune from waterside deals and other rarely spoken about businesses associated with the local unions. It was rumoured that he owned a considerable number of the terraces in The Rocks and Millers Point area, all poorly maintained and cheaply rented out, and all somehow bought at a good price from the Harbour Authority before they were released to the open market. He lived in one at the other end of Kent Street near the Dumbarton Castle Hotel. It was a housing commission place, a derelict sandstone Victorian terrace that was one of the oldest surviving buildings of the first colony and which he rented from the council. How Rowntree merited a housing commission place with all his money was beyond Walker.

'If it's not the Ghost Who Walks,' crowed Bruce Rowntree when he saw him. 'Good to see you, Christopher. Come, take a seat. Reschs as usual or do you drink some poofy bottled shit now you're a doctor?'

'Reschs'll be fine, Bruce.' Walker looked around the bar, which was mostly full of locals, many of whom he recognised. He waved to a few. 'You well?' he asked, turning back to Rowntree.

'Fine, fine. How's the doctoring going? I hear you're at Parramatta or Blacktown or somewhere? Why did they send you all the way out there? Why aren't you at a proper hospital, like Prince Alfred or St Vincent's? Fail some exams, did you?'

'No, you dickhead. The Meadows is the largest teaching hospital in Sydney. Don't you know anything, you stupid prick?' Walker often got the same comments from other acquaintances and it felt good to be frank with Bruce. He wished he could use similar language with the others.

Bruce seemed to accept what he said with a nod of his head. 'But it's cancer you're doing, isn't it?' He put his beer down and bowed forward to present the top of his head. He pointed to a dark raised lesion on his scalp, visible through thinning hair. 'Is this anything to be worried about?'

Walker squinted at it in the dim light. 'Looks like a keratoacanthoma to me.'

Bruce's face fell.

'It's not cancer,' said Walker reassuringly. 'But you shouldn't trust me, I'm an oncologist, not a –'

Bruce brightened up again. 'What about this then.' He pulled the bottom of his shirt out of his pants to show a fat gut. Near the beltline was a raised brownish lump with a cobblestone surface. 'Is it a melanoma?'

'Again,' said Walker, 'I'm an oncologist, not a dermatologist.'

'You're a cancer specialist, aren't you?'

'Yes, but –'

'Well, is it or isn't it? It's a simple question.'

Walker stared down at the lump on the stretched skin of the abdomen, his face twisted in distaste. 'I think it's a seborrheic keratosis.'

'Speak bloody English,' Bruce snapped. 'Is it cancer?'

'No, I don't think –'

'Good.' He pulled his shirt down and frowned. 'See, that wasn't so hard, was it? What do you want from me, my Medicare card?'

Walker shook his head in despair and took a sip of his beer. 'How's business anyway, Bruce?'

Bruce rubbed his bulbous nose and took a gulp of his schooner. 'Oh, you know, up and down – mostly down at the moment. Patrick are really trying to screw the workers.'

Most of the dockside workers in Millers Point were employed by Patrick Stevedores, who were claiming they were becoming unprofitable internationally due to inefficiency and high wages on the Australian wharves.

'Things might get a bit better when the Waterside Workers merge with the Seamen's Union. Hopefully, it'll give us a bit more biffo. Bloody Hawke and Keating are pushing their Accord again, which is all well and good, but some of the members think it's playing into Patrick's hands.'

'Best of luck with all that,' said Walker, which drew a long look from Bruce before he turned back to the bar and took another gulp of his beer.

'What did you want to meet me for?' he growled.

Walker leaned in closer. 'Just wondering whether you're still with the Masons?'

Bruce turned his head. 'Why? You want to join up again? If you do, you have to go all the way this time. I'll not have you playing silly buggers again.'

'No, I don't want to join up. And anyway, I was serious before. I told you, I had to go to New Guinea and didn't have time to finish my degrees.'

'What's to stop you finishing them now?'

'Nothing, I suppose. Too busy at work.' Walker picked up a beer coaster from a stack on the bar and placed his glass on it. "Up The Tooheys Blues" was emblazoned on it. 'Anyway, I'm not ready for that sort of thing yet. After Flea ...' Walker stared blankly down at his beer glass.

Bruce grimaced. 'Yeah, I heard. Tough luck. What happened there, anyway? Heard she drowned. But she was a great swimmer –'

'Bruce, do you mind, I don't want to talk about her.' Walker looked up and down the bar. 'It's about something that happened at work. A doctor was murdered.'

Rowntree pushed a thumb into the side of his bulbous nose. 'And you think the Masons had something to do with it? What sort of a prat are you? Contrary to popular belief, Masons aren't a bunch of secretive murderers –'

'I know that,' Walker interrupted, then continued when Bruce appeared to calm down. 'One of the wardsmen said something about the murdered doctor not making it through his degrees. It sounded to me like a Masonic lodge. He said he was prevented because of his bad character.'

'That'd do it. But was he? The murdered man, was he of bad character?'

'Yes,' said Walker. 'Definitely a bad egg. But also the father of one of my work colleagues. What I want to know is whether you could find out for sure whether he was going through the induction.'

'Probably. Where did he live and what was his name?'

'Epping. His name was Benjamin Chee. And the fellow who knew about it, and is probably a Mason, is Andy Korbmann. Do you want me to write the names down?' He pulled out a pen and paper from his jacket pocket.

'Don't bloody well write anything down,' hissed Bruce, pushing Walker's hand away. 'What have I taught you? I can remember a few names. Or do you think I'm demented or something?' I'll see what I can find out.' He looked at Walker from the corner of his eye as he took a gulp of beer. 'Shirley said you're going to the RAG meeting next Tuesday. I'll meet you there and we can have another talk.'

Walker was about to say he had no intention of attending the Residents Action Group but then he remembered his promise to Shirley the other night in the Hero of Waterloo. He realised Bruce was manoeuvring him to make sure he kept his promise. He sighed. 'Sure, Bruce. Next Tuesday night.'

He drained his glass and looked at it and then at Walker's, his eyebrows raised.

'Two more,' Walker called to the barman.

'What else can I tell you?' said Bruce after he got his beer. 'Did you know I'm thinking of getting into the hotel business? The Dumbarton Castle may be up for grabs. Good pub. Also, you never know, it might be worth something if this new push for development of the area comes to anything. People with money might even want to start living here.'

Walker let out a short laugh. 'Can't see that happening, Bruce. Why would rich people want to live with all of us housing commission lowlifes? But what would I know? I'm one of the lowlifes myself. I'd recommend you don't waste your money.'

Bruce took another sip. 'You're right about one thing. What would you bloody well know? You're a bloody doctor, not a developer.'

Walker could only agree as he drained his glass. 'But I'll eat my hat if the rich ever move into a dumpy suburb like Millers Point.'

'Another one?' asked Bruce, raising his glass.

Walker offered to pay and while they were waiting, Walker asked Rowntree whether there was anything new happening in politics.

'Not much,' he said. 'But,' he rubbed the side of his nose, 'I think Keating's getting a bit antsy about Hawke not passing him the baton.'

'What do you mean? Become prime minister?'

'Exactly.'

'Can he do that?' Walker was genuinely surprised.

Rowntree let out a disparaging snort. 'Bloody hell, Chris! How can you be so clever but also so bloody ignorant about your own government?'

He twisted uncomfortably in his chair. It was true – he had little interest in politics.

'We vote for our local member. And then, in the Labor Party at least, it's the Caucus who votes for their leader. You don't vote in the prime minister. The party can change them if they don't like 'em.'

'I knew that,' Walker said unconvincingly.

Rowntree snorted again as if he didn't believe him. 'Anyway, I bet Keating challenges in the next few months.'

'Have you heard something?'

Rowntree paused before answering. 'No,' he said slowly. 'But I can feel it.' He gulped down the last dregs of his beer and lifted his empty glass. 'Another? My shout.'

## CHAPTER FIFTEEN

WALKER ARRIVED HOME from work early the next evening and had a long shower, making sure he shampooed his hair and cleaned himself up nicely, sniffing his armpits twice to make sure he had expunged all signs of manly odour from his body before he finally hopped out of the old porcelain bathtub. Normally he brushed his hair in about five seconds flat, but tonight he took long minutes, trying out the part in different places and brushing his medium-length hair at the back until he got it just right.

'Maybe I should blow-dry it?' he said, glancing down at the ginger cat that sat just outside his open bathroom door staring up at him. 'What do you think, Archie?' When the cat didn't answer, he gave his unruly locks one more brush on both sides and decided to accept it. 'I need to get myself a better barber.'

His mind drifted to Flea. She used to come with him to the hairdresser to discuss things with the girl as if he were a child and she the mother. But she had very definite ideas on how his hair should look and he had been happy to go along with it. Now that Flea was gone, he'd resorted to going to the local barber and just accepted whatever he got. He pushed her from his mind.

Next, he selected his best pair of Bonds briefs and slipped them on then moved to the hallway to look at himself in the long mirror attached to the outer side of his bedroom door.

He was still in good shape, although there was the beginning of a tummy just above the elastic. His thigh muscles were still strong and his legs were lean and he allowed himself to take a fake-but-stylish ballet position, bending his knees out to the sides before prancing up into the air, almost bashing his head on the low ceiling.

He turned obliquely to further examine his reflection then slapped his tummy. 'I've still got it,' he murmured to himself. Archie took that moment to chirp in his general direction, a uniquely Siberian trait, which Walker decided to take as an affirmation of his opinion. He dressed quickly, putting on a pair of high-waisted blue jeans and a plain T-shirt with a grunge flannel shirt unbuttoned over the top. He finished off the look by slipping on his favourite leather motorbike boots before clattering down the timber stairs.

He grabbed a beer from the fridge, twisting the top off with a flourish, pleased with the power of his grasp. He was feeling good. He was feeling fit. He took a swig of the beer.

He was feeling nervous.

He hadn't been out with a woman since Flea died six years ago. He wandered into the front room and peeked out between the curtains onto Lower Fort Street – nothing except a few youngsters heading down the road towards The Rocks. It was a sultry Friday night and the pubs would already be filling up.

Walker checked himself in the mirror over the mantelpiece yet again. He thought he looked nervous. He tried smiling but that only made it worse.

Archie wandered into the room and lay down near the door, pretending to ignore him.

'This isn't really a date, Archie.'

Walker knew the cat was listening to him. It had taken a while for him to get used to the expressionless feline face; he'd always had a dog. For a while Walker had wondered, with their flat deadpan faces, whether all cats had some sort of neurological condition – something like Parkinson's disease or maybe Asperger's. But now he understood the meaning of a subtle flick of the tail, the squint of the eye or twitch of an ear. Archie was listening all right.

'She's just paying off a wager. I won a bet and she owes me a cup of coffee.' He frowned, realising that coffee was probably the last thing they would drink on a warm Friday night in Sydney in late January. Walker pointed an admonishing finger at the fluffy ginger cat. 'And I'll be getting my coffee, don't you worry about that.'

Just then there was a knock at the door.

'Shit!' he exclaimed and looked at himself in the mirror one last time. He took a deep breath. 'I don't think I'm ready for this.'

Angela looked stunning, there was no other word for it, and with rising despair, Walker realised he was completely out of his league. She wore a short black dress, tight over slim hips, with a top of tight gold-and-silver fabric. Her lean legs were bare and she wore black high heels and carried a tiny silver handbag that matched her dress. Her dark lustrous hair was unadorned and worn long, pulled over one shoulder. Her lipstick was bright red and Walker had to resist kissing them, then and there, on the front doorstep.

Instead, he stumbled backwards and blurted out, 'So you made it then,' or something equally inane. He had to stop himself from staring at her body, her long tanned legs, her bright red lips, and instead focused on her dark brown eyes. But now that also felt unnatural, as if he was some lunatic trying to burrow into her brain. He turned away.

Bloody hell! This is not going well.

'Do I look okay?' She sounded worried and he turned back to her.

'No! You look fantastic! I mean, very nice. You look lovely.'

Now she smiled meekly. 'I thought I might have overdressed.'

He looked down at his grungy clothes and her mouth went wide in consternation as she raised a slender hand. 'I didn't mean ...'

He looked at his clothes again and then at her and then the cat. Then he let out a laugh. Angela frowned prettily.

'I'm sorry, Angela, I'm being an idiot. To be honest, you look absolutely beautiful. I'll try to stop making a fool of myself. It's just that I'm nervous.'

Now she was smiling widely. 'Me too.'

He took a step towards her. 'Let's start again.' He gave her a kiss on the cheek. 'You look beautiful. Thank you for coming.'

She remained in the doorway smiling, now with her hands clasped before her, holding her handbag. 'I'm glad you asked me. Where are we going?'

Walker strode through the front door of the Hero of Waterloo with Angela on his arm, and when heads turned, he felt like a million dollars. He waved to Shirley, seated in her usual spot sipping white wine, and made his way to the bar. James the barman peered over the heads of the crowd waiting to order, took one look at Angela then gave Walker an exaggerated wink, which secretly pleased Walker even more. He was pretty sure that he was with the most beautiful woman in the pub.

They reached the bar and James handed Walker his usual schooner of pilsener. 'And for you, darling?' he asked Angela.

'A chardonnay, please.'

'This is Angela, one of my work colleagues,' said Walker.

'Work colleague,' said James, raising an eyebrow. 'It looks to me like you two are on a date.'

'Oh no,' said Walker quickly. 'I won a bet. She owes me ...' He trailed off, realising how ridiculous he sounded. He turned to Angela, who wore a puzzled expression. 'Is this a date?' he asked her. She shrugged her shoulders and looked uncomfortable. 'I suppose this is a date,' he added.

## Murder on the Ward

'Suppose so,' said Angela but she didn't look happy.

Blast! He was handling this badly.

He led Angela to a small room off the main bar area where there were a few empty tables. They were about to take their seats when a female voice called out from the corner.

'Angela! Chris!'

Seated at the corner table was Cassandra Hollow, looking like a model in a white long-sleeved dress that was very short, showing almost every inch of her very long legs.

'Cassie,' said Angela as she walked towards her. 'You didn't tell me ...'

Cassandra's eyes flicked to the figure who was seated opposite her, facing away from them. He turned.

'Wendy!' exclaimed Walker. 'What are you doing here?'

'Detective Darling?' said Angela with a questioning look at her friend.

'We got talking about the case,' said Cassandra, 'and one thing led to another. Barry and I have promised not to talk about the case tonight. Don't worry, Angela – client confidentiality and all that. This is pure fun.'

Barry Darling beamed up at Walker and gave him a wink.

'Fun?' said Walker, his voice like stone.

'Good to see you two talking again,' said a voice over Walker's shoulder. James stood there with a stack of empty glasses. 'Never knew what you two were fighting about but whatever it was, must have been pretty bad.' He smiled at Angela. 'The Disney Twins we used to call them.'

Walker flashed a look at the barman. 'James, why, out of all the years I've been coming here, have you picked this night to become talkative?'

James jerked a thumb towards Cassandra. 'Is this one of your colleagues as well?' he said dryly. 'I think I might have to come and visit you at work one day.'

Walker put a hand on his shoulder and pointed him towards the door. 'Thanks, James, that will be all. I'm sure there are tables out there that need clearing.'

'Will you join us, Angie?' said Cassandra. 'It'll be nice.'

She looked uncertainly at Darling, who appeared equally uncomfortable.

'No, I don't think that's right,' Walker intervened. 'Anyway, we were just leaving.'

He grabbed Angela's glass and placed it along with his on an empty table, and then motioned for her to leave through the side door out onto Lower Fort Street. As they were leaving, they heard Cassandra call out, 'Have fun you two.'


Out on the footpath, Angela stopped, appearing stunned, so Walker grabbed her around the waist and gently moved her away from the pub. The air was heavy and humid, and in the distance came the deep rumble of thunder.

'Come, Angela, I know another little place we can go to. Phillip's Foote. Nice steaks.'

As they turned into Argyle Street it began to rain – plump intermittent drops at first, but it quickly turned into a teeming downpour, causing them to run to the protection of the sandstone arch of the Argyle Cut. Angela hung onto Walker's arm as she pitter-pattered along in her heels.

'Why would Cassie do that?' asked Angela when they reached the arch. On both sides, fierce rain drummed across the surface of the bitumen, quickly forming rivulets to fill the gutters with a raging torrent.

'You know your friend better than me. But I know Barry Darling. He wouldn't give up a pair of nice legs for any threat of a breach of code of conduct.'

'Can lawyers and police get together socially when they are working on opposite sides of a case?'

'Beats me. But ethics was never one of Wendy's strengths.'

'Police! Do you think all this talk of corruption is true? The papers are full of it. Roger Rogerson and all that.'

'Some of it must be. But I wouldn't say Wendy was corrupt. I don't think it's in his character. Stupid and naive is a better description.'

Angela giggled and Walker felt better. He had started off the evening feeling like a fool but he figured things might be improving. He just had to get through the rest of the evening and not put his foot in it or act like a boor. He grimaced to himself. The odds weren't good. He wasn't used to this sort of thing – socialising with women, trying to be clever and witty.

He'd grown up with Flea, and they just came together as if it was natural. He didn't have to woo her or impress her. In fact, he couldn't remember consciously doing anything to get her to marry him. He couldn't even remember whether he actually proposed to her. They just seemed to belong together and they were happy. It had all seemed so effortless.

And then she died.

Angela was looking at him curiously. 'What are you thinking about?'

'Nothing.' He blew out a large breath. 'Just thinking how hard this all is. All this trying to impress.'

She took a step towards him and put her hands on his waist. The rain battered down like a waterfall on both sides of the arch, locking them in their own little world.

'How about you don't try.' And she leaned forward and kissed him, her moist, red lips thick on his for a tantalising moment before she pulled away, just when he realised what was happening. 'You impress me enough as it is already. Tonight, I'd like just plain normal.'


Twenty minutes later, with the rain stopped, they were at Phillip's Foote, an old-style restaurant in a sandstone colonial building on George Street at The Rocks. At the front was a bar and out back were areas where you could cook your own steak. Walker led Angela to an intimate table in a corner of the garden, the flagstones still wet from the rain and the air thick with the scent of jasmine. He got a Hunter Valley shiraz from the bar and they had fun cooking their steaks, him pretending to be a German tourist and her playing the part of a young girl from the backstreets of Penang. Walker's schoolboy German was atrocious but Angela's Malaysian slang seemed flawless, although incomprehensible to the German, and soon they were falling into each other's arms with laughter as their steaks burned on the grill.

'Why does Detective Darling call you Kit?' asked Angela, soon after they sat down to eat.

'Kit?' Walker gave a short laugh, although there was not much humour in it. 'Stupid name.' He took a sip of his wine as he stared into the distance, thinking of another time. 'Barry Darling was a "Phantom Phreak",' he grimaced. 'Spelled with a "ph" not an "f". It was the Australian fan club.'

Angela smiled.

'Well, the Phantom's real name was Christopher Walker.'

'You're kidding.'

'No. The first Phantom vowed to avenge his father who was killed by pirates.' Walker put his fist on his heart. '"I devote my life to the destruction of piracy, greed, cruelty and injustice, and my sons and their sons shall follow me",' he recited. 'And since then, every son has had the same name – Christopher Walker, or Kit Walker.' He raised his eyebrows. 'Thus, my nickname.'

'You seem to know a lot about it.'

Walker was embarrassed. 'Well, I was in the club for a while. We had to swear to fight on the side of the weak against the oppressor.' He looked up and shrugged meekly. 'And all that sort of stuff.'

'Really? Did you have secret handshakes and things like that?'

He squirmed in his seat. 'Not handshakes. We had rings. I had one. Two actually. But Barry was much more into it than me.' He became thoughtful. 'Especially after I got together with Flea. Sometimes I think it was that and everything about the Phantom – you know, fighting evil and standing up for good – that finally led him into the force.'

'Barry ... Detective Darling was your friend?'

Walker grimaced. 'Used to be. Best friends.' He took another sip and stared blankly, deep in thought. Angela put her hand on his arm.

'Tell me about your wife,' Angela said softly.

'My wife?' said Walker, suddenly defensive.

'How did you meet, how long you were married. That sort of thing.'

Walker relaxed somewhat. Those topics seemed safe, if painful, so he began to tell her about how they'd grown up together in Millers Point, that Flea lived around the corner in Argyle towards the Lord Nelson pub.

'Wendy, Flea and I would knock around together and get up to all sorts of mischief,' Walker said fondly. Once he got started his reminiscences came easily. 'On weeknights in summer we'd go down to the wharves and see the boats being unloaded, then ride our bikes under the bridge and hang around the old guns at Dawes Point, smoking and drinking.'

'Didn't your parents worry about where you were?'

'Well, Darling didn't have parents – he's an orphan – and Flea's parents were druggies, out of it most of the time. And me – well my mum had died and my dad was mostly working. As long as I didn't get in trouble with the law, he was happy.'

'And did you? Get in trouble with the law?'

Walker grimaced again. 'A few times. A lot of times, actually. Stealing more than a few times.' He bit his bottom lip. 'Wendy and I stole a car. The cops caught us after a chase. Sergeant Bowles – he was a good guy – hauled us back to The Rocks cop station. In the end, he didn't charge us but gave us a warning. Next time we'd be in juvenile detention, he said. I believed him. Wendy would have been shipped off to Cobham for sure. Juvenile Justice Centre,' he added when he saw her questioning look. 'It was after that that we changed. We pissed off,' he paused apologetically, ' detached ourselves from the crowd we'd been hanging with, and we made a pact that we would make something of ourselves.' He threw his hands up. 'And so here we are – me a doctor, Wendy a cop.'

'And Flea?'

Walker answered slowly. 'She was with me. Wendy didn't like that but there it was.' He took a long swig of his red wine, still with a faraway look in his eye.

'Chris,' said Angela softly. 'How did your wife - Flea - die?'

Walker flicked his focus back, his eyes boring into hers. 'I don't want to talk about that.'

'Was it an accident? Did she get an illness?'

He shifted in his chair but said nothing.

'In New Guinea? You said you were in New Guinea.'

'Yes,' he hissed. 'New Guinea. She died in the highlands of New Guinea.' He looked at his watch. 'Anyway, it's getting late. I think we better get going.'

'Chris, please don't be upset. I'm sorry I pried. We don't have to end the night like this. It's been so lovely.'

He stood abruptly. 'Sorry, Angela, I've got a lot of things to do early tomorrow. Are you okay to drive? I'll walk you back to your car.'


Walker was in his office when Angela came in, closing the door behind her. She had things for him to sign, she said. She'd only been there half an hour before. She had been sitting at his desk working on his computer, and he had leaned over her shoulder to see what she was doing, his mouth close to her ear when he spoke. He'd rubbed his cheek against her jet-black hair as he pulled away, breathing in her scent.

She had left, but now she was back and when she leaned forward to place the papers on his desk, her top billowed open, the top buttons undone to show a bright blue bra tight over small breasts. Now she was beside him and she leaned in close, brushing her chest against his shoulder as she pointed to the places where he had to sign, red fingernails tracing circles.

She came upright slowly and stood there as he swivelled in his chair. Her top was awry with one blue bra cup showing clearly.

'You seem to have come apart there,' he said.

She didn't bother to look down but instead slipped her red-tipped finger behind her blouse and stroked the top of her breast. 'Oh? Can you do anything about it?'

He looked at her for some moments as if contemplating what to do.

'Take off your panties.'

Angela seemed surprised and stopped caressing herself but her hand slipped to her side. Then slowly, slowly, her hands pinched up the billowing green paisley skirt until the hem was level with her crotch. Smoothly, her hands moved under the skirt as she hooked her thumbs over the top of her panties and slid them off, letting them fall to the ground around her feet.

'Give them to me,' he said.

She stooped and picked them up and he took them and placed them in his top drawer, closing it tight shut.

'Now sit on my lap.'

She swivelled and put one hand on his shoulder and moved to sit sideways. 'Not like that,' he told her. 'Face me.'

She straddled him, pushing against him, hard, both hands on his shoulders. She leaned in and kissed him and her hands joined together behind his neck, pulling him in. He moved his hands under her skirt and cradled her thighs in his hands. She squirmed and he pushed his tongue into her mouth. She groaned and pulled away.

Now she was smiling at him, Flea, his wife. She looked at him with such deep love in her eyes and she kissed him again.

Again, she pulled away. But now her eyes were strange. Dead. Lifeless.

'I have to go,' she said, her voice flat.

'Go! Why?'

She stood up and he blinked his eyes in disbelief. When he opened them, she was gone.

He jolted upright in bed, gasping for air.

'Flea!' He looked desperately around his room – his bedroom. Not his office. Relieved, he flopped back down on the bed.

'A dream,' he grunted. 'It was just a dream, Flea.' He rolled towards her to tell her of it.

But she was not there.

Then the Black came again, surging up from his guts, pulling him into it.

She was gone.

Flea.

Dead.

He tried to picture her face but now he was awake, he couldn't.

He never could.

He had forgotten what she looked like.

Except in his nightmares.

Only then could he see her.

He began to sob.

## CHAPTER SIXTEEN

THAT WEEKEND THE Black took over. Walker spent the nights fighting his dreams and the days lying on the lounge, drinking beer. He ate nothing except a packet of Jatz and didn't wash. He failed to go to work on the Monday, calling up in the morning to tell one of the secretaries he had an upset stomach.

At midday, there was a knock at the door. He ignored it. But whoever it was was insistent and finally, he dragged himself to his feet and opened the door.

Janet, his neighbour, stood there frowning. She was worried about Archie. She hadn't seen him since Friday night.

Walker coughed. 'I've been sick.'

'You look it too. But what have you been feeding him?'

Walker looked at her dumbly. 'Feeding him?' He looked down at his hand in which he clasped a broken Jatz cracker.

With a start, Walker remembered.

Friday evening, he'd walked Angela back to her car, hardly saying a word all the way, and then clumsily gave her a peck on the cheek before helping her into the car. As she drove off, she had crunched the gears of her Honda as it lurched around the corner. He vaguely remembered the aristocratic cat sitting on his front mat like a little motionless sphinx. Archie must have followed him in.

'You can't feed a cat biscuits,' Janet snapped. 'Where is he?'

Just then, Archie trotted up the hallway and out the front door, looking no worse for wear. Walker had no idea where the cat had been.

'I'm so sorry, Janet. I didn't know he was here.'

After she left, Walker dragged himself up the stairs and had a shower, standing under the hot water for half an hour, washing away the Black. He ate, and although he was not feeling much better, he knew he would go to work the next day.

Walker tossed and turned again all night trying to drive images from his mind of Flea grasping uselessly for him in the darkness, her calm, dead face unbreathing, but then laughing at him as if it were all a joke. Later he had woken with the lingering image of Angela smiling at him, her face close to his, holding his head in her hands, telling him that everything was going to be all right.

He turned up late for work and Angela had already started the clinic. She came out of the examination room as he walked in.

'Did you get home safely on Friday?' he asked awkwardly.

'Yes, thank you,' she said without emotion and then immediately launched into business. She didn't ask about his sickness. 'Mr Bob Caldwell is having problems. His colon cancer has relapsed twelve months after adjuvant 5FU and levamisole. The CT shows multiple liver metastases. I've just broken the news to him and his wife but I think you should see them.'

There followed a difficult thirty minutes of explanation and discussion as to why (how!) the cancer could have come back. The surgeon said he got it all. The chemotherapy was just an insurance policy. How could the cancer come back now? Or was it a new cancer? Are you sure it is cancer? Do I need more surgery? Can't you just cut it all out?

When they had finally got down to the miserable options of treatment and prognosis, the wife was crying and the patient was sitting stoically trying to comfort her. They had finally left with an appointment for a fine-needle aspiration of

## Murder on the Ward 121

the liver lesions by radiology in a few days, and a promise to talk more about it when they got the results next week.

The remainder of the clinic was not much better. Patients with new diagnoses of various cancers, patients halfway through their chemotherapy and struggling with the side effects, and two others who'd had a recurrence: an older man with the second relapse of small cell lung cancer which could not be treated, and a young mother whose breast cancer had come back with a pleural effusion – a fluid collection on the outside of the lung. They'd struggled through the discussion with her three-year-old son jumping up and down on her lap throughout. She put him down, but then he pushed the chairs over in the room and so they had to end it, agreeing for her to return with her husband and without her child the next day. But she didn't know who she could get to babysit.

By the end of the clinic, Walker felt wrung out, even more than usual, and wasn't looking forward to the ward round of inpatients who were mostly undergoing terminal care for untreatable cancers.

'Do you think this will ever get better?' he groaned to no one in particular after the last patient had left. Could medical science ever make any headway against this unrelenting disease? The oncology nurses who were tidying up after the clinic looked at him as if he was being foolish.

'You're the doctor, Dr Walker, not us. You tell us.'

Then one of the nurses nudged her friend and smiled cheekily. 'But on a more interesting topic, we hear that you and Angela went out for dinner last Friday. How was it?' She leered suggestively then repeated it when Angela walked in on them.

'It was very pleasant,' Angela said stiffly then turned around and left.

The nurses smirked at each other, then at Walker. 'Bombed out, did you, Chris?' said one. 'Don't worry, you're probably just a bit rusty.' She grinned at her friend. 'And she's probably just a bit shy. Probably a virgin by the look of her. Do you need a few pointers?'

'No, thanks,' he said sourly. 'I'm fine. I better get up to the ward.'

Walker made his way up to the cancer ward in a bad mood. He needed to get away early since he had promised to go to the Resident Action Group meeting at Millers Point, firstly to Shirley at the Hero of Waterloo, and then Bruce Rowntree at the Captain Cook. He really didn't feel up to a public meeting and he considered not turning up. But Rowntree was going to give him some information about Benjamin Chee's involvement with the Freemasons, or at least Walker hoped that would be the case. He had a feeling it had something to do with his murder. But it was just that – a feeling – and so he hadn't shared it with Barry Darling. Darling would have a field day going on about Walker's 'feelings'.

He thought about Darling as he entered the ward. Wendy's a total tosser. I can't believe he's going out with Cassandra. They were on either side of a murder case, for goodness sake.

'Secondly,' said Walker out loud, as he approached the desk, 'she's drop-dead gorgeous and he's a total dipshit.'

'Who's a dipshit?' asked Gloria, seemingly unfazed by his language. Her thick mop of red hair looked like a wig and she had a way of staring stupidly through her thick glasses that made Walker wonder how she got into medicine in the first place. Jenny, the petite nurse, bided her time nearby playing with her fingernails, waiting for them to start the round.

'No one,' Walker said with some irritation. If he'd heard one of his consultants swear when he was an intern, he would have politely pretended he hadn't and not pry into his thoughts. 'Any admissions overnight?'

'Just one,' said Gloria, glancing down at her notes. 'But we should wait for Angela. I'll page her.'

'Don't bother,' said Walker. But to his further irritation, Gloria went ahead and paged her anyway. When she put the phone down, he snapped at her. 'Let's start. I don't have long.'

A moment later Angela turned up, accompanied by Sandy, and they appeared to be in an animated conversation but stopped abruptly when they saw Walker. He wondered if it was only patients they'd been talking about.

'Good morning, boss,' called out Sandy. 'Just in time. We have everything ready.'

'Boss?'

'I'm trying it out. Saw it on *MASH*.'

'Forget it,' said Walker. He pointed up the corridor. 'Lead the way. And, Gloria, I want you to present the patients.'

Gloria reached the first patient, appearing flustered. She flicked through a wad of paper pulled from the large pocket of her white coat, dropping a few of the sheets onto the vinyl floor, which Sandy bent to pick up for her. She pushed her horn-rimmed glasses onto her nose and read from her notes, constantly flicking from page to page as if they were out of order. 'Mr Eaton is sixty-five and has ... er ... small cell lung cancer and was admitted with pneumonia. He has become afebrile on ampicillin and erythromycin but his chest X-ray is no better.' She looked up uncertainly. 'I wonder whether we should change his antibiotics.'

Walker waved to the patient, cast a rapid eye over him and looked at the chart. 'Small cell lung cancer? Are you sure?'

Gloria flicked through a few pages and then, apparently not finding what she wanted, nodded emphatically. 'Yes, I'm quite sure. Small cell lung cancer.'

Walker's voice was kind. 'Gloria, please have a look at Mr Eaton's fingers.' Walker smiled at the patient. 'Do you mind?'

Eaton held up his hand so all could see that the ends of his fingers were expanded like the end of a drumstick.

'Clubbing,' said Gloria, appearing pleased with herself.

'Correct,' said Walker. 'So, do you wish to revise your diagnosis of small cell lung cancer?'

He looked at the other two. Angela seemed embarrassed and Sandy looked like he wanted to shoot up his hand like an excited child in a classroom. Gloria looked perplexed. She opened her mouth but no words were forthcoming.

'Angela?' He didn't look at her when he asked.

'Clubbing occurs with non-small cell lung cancer and virtually never with small cell.'

'Correct.' Walker still had his attention on Gloria. 'And despite the chest X-ray, do you think Mr Eaton is getting better?'

Now Gloria looked addled. 'Yes?' she said uncertainly.

'Yes, I agree with you. His fever has settled, his pulse is down and he looks well. The chest X-ray improvement won't happen for a week. I wouldn't even have bothered doing it. You must learn to trust your own clinical opinion first. Get confident in your skills. What you think, based on your clinical findings, is usually right. The blood tests and X-rays are to confirm your findings, not to give you the answer. If there is a conflict between your diagnosis and the investigations, believe your own opinion first.'

'Okay,' said Gloria, although she looked far from convinced.

'Continue the same antibiotics and let's get Mr Eaton home tomorrow.' Walker shook the patient's hand while Sandy scribbled a note in the file and they moved on.

As they came out of the room, they found the way to the next one was blocked by a hospital bed with Andy Korbmann at one end. The bed was filled with a large lady who seemed unconscious, a number of IV lines disappearing under the bed covers. A nurse stood beside the bed pushing the IV stand on which two blue IMED pumps were attached. The alarm was beeping on one but everyone ignored it.

'We're rejigging a few rooms,' Andy called over his shoulder. 'Shouldn't be too long.'

Walker and his team clustered together in the corridor, unable to get past. Gloria and Sandy stood together, struggling with the pile of notes, and Angela frowned down at a sheet of paper that listed the names of their inpatients. Walker had the feeling she didn't want to talk to him. He felt the same. He looked at his intern and felt as if he might have been too hard on her. It couldn't be easy becoming a doctor so late in life. Maybe he should say something? Show a bit of interest.

'Gloria, what did you do before you became a doctor?'

Her eyes, already magnified by her thick glasses, swelled even further. 'Me?' She looked like a wallaby caught in a pair of headlights.

*No, the* other *Gloria*, he felt like saying. Instead, he tried to soften his voice. 'Did you have another job?' He found it difficult to sound reasonable when she irritated him so much.

'Well, I ... I worked as a set designer.'

'A set designer,' said Angela, looking up. 'That's very interesting.'

'A set designer?' blurted Walker. He realised he sounded rude but he couldn't believe the drab intern could have done anything so artistic.

Gloria's body seemed to shrink and she looked from Angela to Walker as if they didn't believe her. 'Yes, for some years,' she mumbled. 'But I didn't like it.' Then she pointed. 'Oh look. The corridor is clear now. We should get on.' She led the way into the next room and stopped at the first bed.

In it sat a middle-aged man who Walker thought he recognised but couldn't quite place. He looked completely healthy and out of place in the cancer ward.

'Mr Aaron Young,' said Gloria and Walker gave her a blank look.

Angela intervened. 'We saw Mr Young in the clinic just the other day. Stage one testicular cancer.'

'Ah, yes, of course,' said Walker, remembering all the details now that he had a point of reference. 'Embryonal carcinoma with normal markers and no vascular invasion, low chance of recurrence on the surveillance program.' He frowned. 'What are you doing in hospital?'

'Funny turn,' said Gloria. She glanced down at her notes. 'Wife says she found him staring blankly into space. Couldn't get any sense out of him and brought him to Emergency. When he arrived, he was as he is now. Completely alert and nothing wrong. But the wife refused to take him home.' She smirked. 'We are getting social work to see the wife. I think she's a bit overwrought.'

Walker scratched his chin. 'Doesn't seem right.' He addressed the patient. 'Aaron, I remember you said you were getting funny smells. Are you still getting them?'

'Yes, as a matter of fact. I was in my office and got this distinct burnt coffee smell. Then things seemed to go blank and the next thing I knew I was in hospital.' He shook his head. 'I must have fainted.'

'I don't think you fainted,' said Walker. He raised his eyebrows at Angela.

'It could be,' she said, nodding. 'We'll organise an EEG.'

'An electroencephalogram,' said Sandy. 'Why?'

'Could be absence fits. Petit mal,' said Angela. 'But there was the olfactory prodrome – the unusual odours.'

'What are you talking about?' said Aaron. 'Sounds bad. Some sort of fit?'

'Sounds like it,' said Walker. 'The funny smells are part of the fits. The part of the brain involved with smell was firing off. But not sure why you would start getting them now. They usually start at a much younger ...'

Walker stopped and looked at the patient. Aaron Young was staring ahead with a blank expression. He started to chew as if he had a mouth full of cud. Then his left arm began to jerk.

Aaron fell back onto the bed, his back arched, and all of his limbs jerked in unison, his arms contracting and extending and his legs twitching.

'He's fitting!' yelled Gloria. 'Call the arrest team.'

'Don't call an arrest,' Walker said to Jenny who was moving out of the room. 'Turn him onto his side.'

Sandy and Angela carefully rolled the patient onto his side and held him there as his limbs continued to jerk rhythmically, his back arched.

'Do we have to stop him swallowing his tongue?' squawked Gloria.

'He's just having a fit,' Walker said calmly. 'He'll stop in a moment. We just need to prevent him from hurting himself.'

'But he's not breathing!' she shouted.

Aaron's arms and legs continued to jerk in and out rhythmically although the rate was slowing. Jenny put a mask over his mouth and nose and turned on the oxygen.

'Shouldn't we give him a Valium injection or something?' said Gloria, her voice shrill. She was shaking her head and grasping the bedend as if that action would somehow help.

'Haven't you seen a fit before?' said Walker. 'Almost all stop on their own accord. Just calm down, Gloria, you're overreacting.'

'It's just terrible to watch,' she gasped.

'Well, you're going to see a lot worse than this in your career,' said Walker. 'Get used to it. If you don't like it, leave the room.'

Gloria glared at her consultant, breathing hard, but she stayed put.

Soon the jerking stopped and Aaron began to breathe deeply as if he had just run a fast race. Soon he was breathing steadily but remained unconscious.

'Shall we start some phenytoin?' asked Angela.

'Sure,' said Walker. 'Give him three hundred milligrams. We'll need a CT scan of his brain. We may as well give him a steroid injection just in case.'

'Brain secondaries from the testis cancer?' asked Sandy.

'I doubt it,' said Walker. 'Stage one testicular cancer does not spread to the brain without spreading to other places first. He only had a CT of his chest and abdomen last week and that was clear, as were his blood tumour markers. Testicular cancer is very predictable.'

'What is it then?' asked Angela.

'Not sure at this stage. We'll wait to see what the tests show but I wouldn't be surprised if the brain scan is clear.'

A short time later, Walker was leaning against the nurses' station bench waiting for his team to return from their duties regarding Aaron Young. Jenny had given the patient the intravenous steroid injection and Aaron, who was starting to wake up, had already been wheeled off to radiology for the brain scan, accompanied by Sandy. Nearby, Angela was speaking to the radiology registrar on the phone and Gloria had disappeared somewhere in a fluster.

'I hear you've been off sick. Are you okay?' Jenny asked quietly.

'Ah. It was nothing.' He patted his belly. 'Tummy bug.'

She smirked as if she didn't believe him. 'How did you go with Angela?'

Walker carefully examined her face for any signs of amusement but found none and realised she was honestly interested.

'Good up to a point,' he muttered, careful so that Angela wouldn't overhear. 'We had fun at the restaurant but it ended badly.'

Jenny raised her eyebrows.

'She was prying about Felicity.'

The petite nurse mouthed a silent 'Oh' then glanced at Angela. When Jenny saw she was still in conversation on the phone she turned back to him. 'The great mortal sin! Asking the impenetrable Dr Christopher Walker about his late wife. How could she?' she said with mock dismay.

For some reason, when Jenny spoke about Felicity it didn't bother him. He'd thought hard about it before and figured it was the fact that she didn't seem at all interested in finding out the details of his wife's death. Mostly they spoke about the effect on *him*, which was different to everyone else, who wanted to know the gory details, with no thought of how recounting the circumstance of his wife's death might affect him.

'Exactly,' said Walker, choosing to ignore her sarcasm.

She moved closer and dropped her voice. 'Chris, you know you will have to speak about it to anyone you want to get close to.'

'Why?' he said sharply. 'It'll have nothing to do with them – whoever it is. I respect people's privacy. I wouldn't pry into someone else's life.'

Jenny shrugged. 'I wouldn't trust a person who didn't open up to me. I'd wonder how many other secrets he had.'

'Well, you must have a perfect marriage then, Jenny,' snapped Walker. But he instantly regretted his words and raised a hand. 'Sorry, that was rude of me. I know you're only trying to help.'

But Jenny didn't seem to have taken offence. 'Don't worry, Chris. I've been a cancer nurse for over ten years. You'll have to say a lot worse than that to upset me.'

Then Walker noticed that Andy Korbmann was hovering nearby. He had the distinct impression the wardsman was listening to their conversation while he pretended to read a pamphlet tacked to the noticeboard on the wall of the nurses' station. It had small photos of all the current interns with their names' underneath. Andy appeared to be studying it.

'Thought you'd know all the interns by now, Andy,' said Walker.

'Just checking,' he said. 'Besides, some haven't worked here yet.' The interns rotated through other hospitals and many had started their year elsewhere. 'You don't know who'll show up in unusual places.'

'What do you mean?'

He moved closer and dropped his voice. 'Just talking about seeing people in places you didn't expect them.'

'Say what you mean, Andy,' said Jenny.

He looked around and then back to the pair. 'It's just that Professor McBrent has been poking around the coronary care unit.'

'McBrent,' said Walker with interest 'So? He was probably consulting a patient.' McBrent was an endocrinologist and would rarely need to attend the CCU. Walker understood what Andy was hinting at. Professor Chee had been killed by an overdose of metoprolol, a drug commonly used in the coronary care unit.

'I'm pretty sure he wasn't seeing a patient.'

Walker was silent for a few moments as he studied Andy and wondered why he was giving him this information.

'Have you told the police?'

'I thought you might, Dr Walker. You seem to be good friends with the detective.'

'I'm not,' Walker snapped. 'Did you see him take anything?'

'Can't say I did,' said Andy. 'But I did wonder.' He looked around again and then back at Jenny and finally Walker. 'He was Professor Chee's consultant, after all. And it was the day before his death that I saw Professor McBrent in CCU.'

Walker grunted. It sounded to him as if Andy was trying to set McBrent up. Or maybe he was just reporting what he had honestly seen? 'Okay, I'll tell Detective Darling when I see him. But I will also tell him where I got the information from.'

Andy smiled, appearing unconcerned, before wandering off.

'What do you think about that?' Walker asked Jenny as he stared at Andy's back.

'Beats me,' said Jenny. 'Does sound suspicious though. And McBrent's a creep. I wouldn't put it past him.'

# CHAPTER SEVENTEEN

WALKER REACHED THE hall of the Garrison Church just as the RAG meeting was beginning. Up front stood Shirley the chairperson, sour-faced and silver-haired. The seats in the hall were full, with an eclectic mix – businessmen in suits and ties, old women in tracksuits, overweight wharfies still in their boilersuits and elegant ladies in flowing dresses and heels. Bruce Rowntree, bald-headed and ruddy-faced and wearing a crumpled suit, was halfway up on the left and he waved to Walker when he entered, pointing to the empty seat beside him. As he sat down, Walker noticed Barry Darling a few rows up.

'I'll call the meeting to order,' said Shirley. 'The first point on the agenda is the continued threat of the sale of properties in Millers Point by the Department of Housing. You all know that we managed to stop the Greiner government from selling the Hero of Waterloo and Harbour View hotels two years ago. You also know they have not given up. Last year they tried to sell the Millers Point shops and the residential flats above the hotels. We also managed to stop that but we must remain vigilant. Alderman Sartor and representatives from RAG met with the department and were told, in no uncertain terms, that the Greiner government has a philosophical commitment to selling commercial properties in our area.' She paused and looked around the room meaningfully, taking off her glasses and allowing them to hang on the lanyard around her neck.

'A philosophical commitment,' she repeated meaningfully, emphasising her words with a stab of a finger. 'That means they won't stop until they get what they want or until they get voted out.'

'That's not going to happen any time soon,' said a young man in a business suit in the front row. 'They won by a landslide in '88. The next election's not due for another eighteen months and they'll have to lose a lot of seats to concede the election.'

'Greiner's on the nose,' countered Shirley. 'His education minister, Tony Metherell, is fighting with the teachers. Greiner has closed down the north coast railway, which has them hopping mad. Opposition leader Bob Carr is trying to pin the recent upswing in car deaths on the Pacific Highway on the increased traffic due to the rail closures. And Greiner's trying to sell off public assets left, right and centre so he's got a lot of people's backs up.

'We must stand firm.

'They can't last forever.

'When Labour gets back in, we'll be safe. But at the moment, all that stands between the outright sale of Millers Point and The Rocks is us, the City of Sydney Council and the unions. The Building Workers are threatening Green Bans. I don't have to remind you how successful they were when the entire Rocks was under threat back in the seventies.'

'The unions are not what they were in the seventies, Shirley,' said the same young man in a suit. 'Bob Hawke's Accord has seen to that.'

'Bloody oath,' Bruce Rowntree said to Walker out of the side of his mouth. 'The Maritime Union will show them what's what.'

'Who are they?' asked Walker, although he immediately regretted asking it. They were getting glares from people in front of them.

'I told you the other night. The Waterside Workers and the Seamen's Union are merging. Then they'll be the Maritime Union. And believe me, they'll pack a punch.'

'Oh,' said Walker, trying to put as much disinterest as he could into the single word in an effort to cut off the discussion.

Rowntree seemed to get the hint since he went back to listening to the discussion.

Shirley was still speaking. 'We also have another government department on our side – the Department of Planning – which in its Millers Point Conservation Study says,' she put her glasses back on and peered down at a pamphlet in her hand, '"Millers Point is an immensely complex interaction between architecture, archaeology, landscape, landform, location, past and present use."' She paused and looked out at the audience again before continuing.

'And that the most significant aspect of the place is its people.' She stabbed her finger again at the pamphlet. 'The people. That's us.' She pointed around the room. 'Every one of us.'

She looked back at the pamphlet. 'And it also said that "the mistakes made in The Rocks should not be repeated here".' She looked up, 'And by God, we won't let it.'

The discussion then turned to the planned development of the wharves of Walsh Bay. The developers had sought an exemption to the Heritage Act so they could demolish the original bond stores to make way for housing.

Rowntree swore under his breath and energetically entered the discussion. 'I suggest we ask for the tendering process to be examined. Let's give Greiner and his flunkies a taste of their own medicine. I vote that we make a submission to the Independent Commission Against Corruption.'

'What's ICAC going to do?' interjected the fellow in the suit in the front row, his face screwed up with contempt.

'You'd be surprised,' said Rowntree. 'They represent the people, not the government.'

The young man folded his arms on his chest and smirked, saying nothing, but giving the impression he thought Rowntree to be naive.

Walker allowed his mind to wander. As far as he was concerned, this is what it had always been like living in The Rocks. Ever since he could remember, the big end of town and the government had been trying to tear down the buildings, kick the housing commission people out of their houses, and build something else. As far as he was concerned, they were fighting a losing battle. Silently, he wondered whether he should move somewhere else.

Somewhere less contentious.

Epping maybe.

He thought about Angela.

He wondered whether she was at the Epping pub. Wondered whether she was meeting young men with Cassandra. The two of them together – dark and blonde – were quite a drawcard.

He bit the inside of his lip. For sure they would have men all around them vying for their attention! What was he thinking?

Soon the meeting was over and people were standing in small groups in the corridors and between the seat rows having their own discussions.

Bruce Rowntree, his legs stretched out in front and arms crossed over his chest, elbowed Walker in the side. 'Come out the front. I need a fag.'

They stood on the sandstone flagging out the front of the church hall. A cool breeze came in from the harbour and the sun had set. Overhead, the fruit bats wheeled and squawked, heading towards the Moreton Bay figs up on Observatory Hill.

Rowntree lit a cigarette and dragged on it then blew the smoke out luxuriously. Down the street, the lights of the Hero of Waterloo could be seen. Walker wished he was there, sipping on a pilsener.

'I found out about this Chee fellow for you,' growled Rowntree through a smoker's cough.

'Oh yes?' said Walker, becoming interested.

'At the Eastwood meeting hall. A fellow called Korbmann was sponsoring him.'

'To join the Masons?'

Rowntree gave him a look and blew smoke out of the corner of his mouth. 'No, to join the local fuckin' church. Of course the Masons, you stupid prick.'

Walker said nothing and waited for Rowntree to continue. Darling stepped out of the hall and saw them immediately. He made to walk towards them but was stopped by Shirley, who engaged him in conversation.

'What did you find?' Walker asked quickly.

'This Professor Chee of yours was a total slimebag. Some sort of sexual deviant. And he had some sort of past in Asia.'

'In Asia? What do you mean?'

'Don't know that,' snapped Rowntree. 'I'm not a fuckin' detective.' He blew out another lungful of smoke. 'But it was all very suspicious and the Masons didn't want a bar of him. Sent him packing. Apparently totally pissed off his sponsor as well, who claimed he knew nothing about it.'

'Korbmann?'

'Yeah, and another bloke. A doctor he worked with.' Before Walker could ask more, Rowntree looked around and let out a rough laugh. 'Here comes your little mate.' Darling was walking towards them and Rowntree raised his voice. 'Whatever happened to you two lovebirds anyway? Thick as thieves you used to be. The Disney Twins.' He gave a phlegmy chuckle. 'I always liked that. And you two had promise in the unions. Why did you both go off and become upright citizens? Never pays, you know.' He turned away as Darling reached them. 'Although Barry here, being a copper, would know nothing about being an upright citizen. Would you, Bazza?'

'Good to see you too, Bruce. How's the bag business going?'

'Listen to this,' said Rowntree, tapping Walker on the chest and throwing his head towards Darling. 'A copper talking to me about being a bagman.' He tossed his head at Darling again. 'Taking lessons off Roger Rogerson are you, Darling? He's just out of the clanger but I don't like his chances of staying out. Still, you'll have a few months at least to pick up his dirty tricks.'

'Bugger off, Bruce. I've never even met the bloke.'

Rowntree blew out a puff of cigarette smoke and began to sidle away. 'You'd better crack on then. Someone's gotta take his place.'

Darling watched calmly as Rowntree walked away. 'Charming as usual.' He turned to Walker. 'What are you doing here?'

Walker tilted his head towards the silver-haired woman who was addressing a circle of businessmen and locals. 'Shirley made me promise.'

Darling laughed. 'Yeah, me too.'

'Wendy,' said Walker, 'I think you should know something about Professor Chee. I got the info from Rowntree. One of the wardsmen at the hospital was helping Chee to join the Masons. But he never made it through the vetting process. Somehow, they found out about his past. Sexual deviances and something he did in Asia,' he added in answer to Darling's raised eyebrows.

'What's the wardsman's name?'

'Andy Korbmann.'

Darling wrote in his notebook. 'I'll speak to him tomorrow.'

'And one more thing. Andy also said that he saw Denis McBrent in the coronary care unit the day before Chee's death.' He continued when Darling gave him a questioning look. 'McBrent's an endocrinologist. And apparently, he didn't have any patients in the CCU.' Darling's face remained blank. 'And the CCU is full of metoprolol.'

'Ah,' Darling said finally. He made a note then he frowned down at his pad. 'Why would Korbmann tell you this?'

'Don't know.'

Darling looked up. 'Thanks for the information.'

Walker shuffled his feet awkwardly. 'No problem. Thought I'd better tell you.'


Detective Sergeant Barry Darling and Senior Constable David Jones came early to the hospital the next morning, having parked in the loading docks at the back of the hospital, close to the clinical departments. They sauntered along the long linoleum-covered corridor of the clinical building, reading the names on each door and occasionally stopping to study the posters on the wall.

They had almost reached the end when a door opened ahead, and into the corridor stepped their person of interest, who strode briskly away from them in the opposite direction.

'Professor McBrent,' Darling called.

The doctor ignored them, not even bothering to pause and see who'd called.

'I'd like to talk to you about Professor Benjamin Chee if you have time,' Darling persisted, walking quickly to catch up with the older doctor.

McBrent half turned and seemed ready to let fly with a round of expletives but paused when he saw the detective's badge and the towering uniformed bulk of Constable Jones.

'I'm terribly busy, I'm sorry,' he barked. 'On my way to give a lecture to the medical students. It'll have to wait.'

Darling glanced at his wristwatch. 'Lecture?' he said pleasantly. 'So that would start at nine o'clock? It's only eight forty-five so you have a few minutes.'

He placed a restraining hand on McBrent's elbow but he pulled away abruptly, neck veins bulging and mouth tight in a sneer, looking as if he would explode. He struggled to control his anger and managed to twist his lips into a semblance of a smile. 'Of course, officer. Anything to help.'

'Let's move over here where we can be alone.'

Off the crush area of the lecture theatres were several small rooms used for tutorials and other small-group meetings and Darling directed McBrent into the closest and closed the door.

'Professor McBrent, what were you doing in the coronary care unit the night before Dr Chee's death?'

McBrent frowned. 'CCU? I wasn't there. Who said I was? Why would I be there? I'm an endocrinologist – that's diabetes and thyroid problems and the like.'

'Thank you, professor, I know what an endocrinologist is.'

McBrent's frown deepened, giving the impression that he greatly doubted the police officer truly knew what an endocrinologist did.

'And that is exactly my question. What would an endocrinologist be doing in the CCU?'

'I wasn't.' McBrent sounded certain.

'We have a witness.'

'Who?' he snapped.

'That's privileged information.' Darling opened his hands and tried to sound apologetic. 'Professor, you know that Benjamin Chee died from an overdose of metoprolol, a drug commonly used in a coronary care unit. We are obliged to track down anything that seems out of the ordinary. And an endocrinologist in a CCU when he has no patients admitted there seems to require explanation.'

McBrent's bloodshot eyes darted from Darling to Jones and back to Darling. 'If I tell you, will you keep it to yourselves?'

'Ourselves?'

'If I tell you why I was there, do you have to record it? Will it become public knowledge?'

'Not unless it has something to do with the murder.'

'You can't let my wife know. She has her own money. But she likes my position – you know, the prestige of having a professor for a husband. It's one thing she has over her friends. Their husbands are all rich businessmen. She likes the

## Murder on the Ward

status.' McBrent opened his hands imploringly. 'You two know what women are like. I don't think she'd understand.'

'Understand what?' asked Darling.

McBrent paused then seemed to come to a decision. 'I was saying hello to one of the nurses.'

'A nurse? Can you give me a name?'

McBrent recited a name and Jones wrote it down.

'Why did you need to see her in the CCU?'

McBrent looked uneasy, his face suddenly turning a rosy hue. He pulled on the neck of his shirt then unbuttoned the top button and loosened his tie. 'You promise this will go no further?'

Darling said nothing.

'Okay then, I'll tell you. But you can't tell my wife.'

Constable Jones raised his eyebrows and waited, his pen poised over the notepad.

'I went there to have sex.'

'Sex?' Darling glanced at Jones. 'In the CCU?'

'Yes. You can check with the nurse.'

Darling looked baffled. 'But where?'

'In one of the beds.'

Jones looked at Darling and back to McBrent. 'Were there other patients in the room?'

Now McBrent did explode. 'No, you knucklehead. The room was a private one and the bed was empty. The patient had been taken in a wheelchair to X-ray. Due for discharge.'

'Not the most romantic of places,' said Jones.

'She owed me a favour,' snapped McBrent. 'And who said it was supposed to be romantic?'

'So, you're having an affair with a nurse?'

'No! Like I said, she owed me a favour. It's categorically *not* an affair.'

'How long were you there?'

'Five minutes, no more.' McBrent pointed his finger as if he had won a point. 'Not enough time to take any metoprolol. Ask her, she'll tell you.'

'Five minutes,' murmured Jones sarcastically. 'Impressive.'

McBrent grunted as if he had been given a compliment. 'But you can't let my wife know. She'll not understand.'

'She'll not understand why you had sex with a nurse or why you only took five minutes?'

McBrent ignored Darling's sarcasm. 'My wife is naive.' He smiled conspiratorially. 'She doesn't understand the way of men. If she found out, she'd read something into it. Like I said, the girl owed me a favour, nothing more.'

'A sexual favour. What did you do for her?' Jones asked with genuine interest.

'I got her father to the top of the list for radioactive therapy for his thyroid. The waiting list is at least six months but she wanted her father treated faster.'

'So you got him to the top of the list if she had sex with you?'

McBrent looked nonplussed. '*She* offered. I would have accepted a bottle of Scotch.' He looked at the two police officers who now seemed dumbstruck. 'Is that all? I have a lecture to give.'

'That will be all, professor. But we *will* check your story.'

McBrent moved towards the door but turned back and glared threateningly. 'Remember, say nothing to my wife. If any of this gets out, I'll know where it came from.'

Jones stared after him, then spoke to Darling. 'What a freak. But you didn't tell him about the photos.'

Darling scratched the back of his head. 'What a sleazebag. Gives men a bad name.' He dropped his voice. 'Let's keep that little secret to ourselves for the moment. I think we should find out a bit more about the professor.'

## CHAPTER EIGHTEEN

BARRY DARLING DRUMMED his fingers on his office desk. There had been a development – information recovered from security camera footage that seemed conclusive. But something had come up, and rather than attending to it personally, he was forced to send Constable Jones off to the hospital to deal with it. That annoyed him.

Why did everything have to happen at once?

He let out an exasperated breath. Just after viewing the camera footage, he'd received a fax saying he would get a call from New Guinea that morning. He really didn't want to miss the call.

The phone rang and he snapped it up.

'Detective Darling, I have Sergeant Martin Kora on the phone from the Royal Papua New Guinea Constabulary in Mount Hagen. He wants to speak to you about your enquiry.'

Darling stood swiftly and turned to the window. 'Put him through.'

Sergeant Kora had a young-sounding voice with a New Guinean accent and spoke excellent English. 'Port Moresby said you wanted information about Christopher Walker. I know him. I was involved with his case in '85. Terrible thing. What would you like to know?'

'I don't really know anything about it. I hear Walker's wife died.'

'Can I ask what this is about?'

Darling paused. What could he say? It had to be more than curiosity on his part. More than self-interest in finding out about the death of a woman he'd admired. 'I'm investigating a murder here in Sydney. Walker is involved.'

'Walker involved in a murder? Strange, he didn't seem the type. Granted, he was in no fit state when we found him. Half delirious, talking all sorts of nonsense.'

'Where did you find him?'

'In a village in the Eastern Highland province, south of Goroka. There were stories filtering through of a white man and woman who had drowned down near Eteve. That's in the middle of nowhere, I can tell you. A hard day's drive from Mount Hagen, then some. Finally, we got word from one of the missionaries that it was true. I was the junior officer so I got the job of checking it out. The Goroka police really should have gone but they were out searching for another missing Australian. A geologist. So I had to go. Bloody long trip but sure enough, there was a white man there, all right. It was Walker. I found him in one of the huts another day's walk south of Eteve on the other side of the river. One of the old women had been looking after him. Most of the village had moved on to farm further north and she had been left to care for him.'

'What was he like?'

'A total mess. Clothes gone, skin and bone, and out of his mind. His wife had drowned, you see. They'd got caught in a flash flood while they were travelling up the river to Misapi Mission. He'd been laying in that hut in the jungle for more than a month before we got to him.'

'His wife drowned. Are you sure of that?'

'Well, the locals said she had drowned along with their guide. I had no reason to disbelieve them. Walker looked like he had almost drowned himself. Lucky to be alive. Lucky he didn't die of infection afterwards. He was in a terrible state. Didn't know where he was, talking nonsense. We had to fly him out from Gimi, and when we finally got him back to

Mount Hagen it took a few more weeks to get any sense out of him.'

'Was the wife's body ever found?'

'No, although we didn't look too hard. The terrain there is rugged, let me tell you.'

There was silence on the phone as Darling brooded over the officer's answers.

Kora asked, 'What's the murder in Sydney about? Do you think Walker did it?'

Darling was roused from his thoughts about Felicity. 'Walker? No, I don't think he's involved in the murder.' At least not this one, thought Darling. 'Thanks for calling me, Sergeant Kora. Do you mind if I call you again if I have any questions?'

'Please,' he said, 'call me Martin. Call again by all means. And if you are ever up in PNG, come up to Mount Hagen. The Australian officers are always interested in what we do on our jungle patrol. It's tough up here, but you know how it is.' There was a pause. 'We stand against evil.'

'Of course,' said Darling and hung up. He glanced down at the notes he'd taken while talking on the phone. Misapi Mission. Gimi. Eteve. He'd never heard of them. 'Drowned in a river,' he said aloud. Did they even travel on the river in that part of PNG? Then he realised the officer hadn't mentioned a boat. Maybe they'd been walking up the stream. Darling realised he still did not have a good picture of the events surrounding Felicity's death. He'd been unprepared and he promised himself he would make a list of questions and call the officer at another time.

Darling stared out of his window, deep in thought. There was the other thing Kora had said. *We stand against evil.* And he had mentioned the jungle patrol. Darling let out a short laugh.

Sergeant Martin Kora was a Phantom Phreak.

Senior Constable Jones was waiting in the office when Walker came out of the clinic room. The young uniformed policeman was accompanied by a diminutive female officer with a large gun in her holster, which emphasised her small stature.

'I'm after Angela Chee,' Jones said without preamble.

'What for?'

'None of your business, Dr Walker.' He flicked his head towards the row of doors that lined the corridor. 'Is she in there?'

'She shouldn't be long. She's seeing a cancer patient.' Walker threw the file he was holding down onto the bench. 'Can't this wait until after the clinic? We have a lot of patients.'

Jones's reply was short. 'No.' He folded his arms over his chest and stared towards the doors, his face expressionless.

One of the nurses addressed the female officer. 'Didn't you used to be a nurse?'

The policewoman smiled. 'Yeah, I worked in Casualty.'

'Not enough blood and guts?' laughed the nurse. 'So you had to become a copper to see some more.'

'Something like that.' But her smile faded at the curt glance Jones gave her and her expression became serious as she stared up the corridor, her lips tight.

The nurses made faces at each other then went back to their duties.

Presently, Angela came out of one of the rooms and slowed when she saw the officers. Jones walked towards her, the female officer at his side. Angela halted and looked over their shoulders at Walker.

She looked afraid.

'Angela Walker,' intoned Jones. 'You are under arrest for the murder of Benjamin Chee. I am Senior Constable Jones from the Parramatta station and this is Constable Green.'

Angela seemed to physically slump. One hand went to her chest and the arm holding the patient file fell by her side. She looked like she might faint.

'You are not obliged to say or do anything unless you wish to do so,' Jones continued. 'But whatever you say or do may be used in evidence. Do you understand?'

Angela nodded, the colour drained from her face.

'What are you talking about?' Walker demanded. He tried to push past but Jones barred his way with a muscular forearm.

'Piss off, Walker,' he barked. 'I still owe you one for what you did to Detective Darling in the docks. Just give me an excuse.'

'Bugger off, Jones, you big oaf.' Walker gave him a shove. 'What proof do you have?'

Jones thumped Walker up against the plaster wall. There was a clatter as something on the other side of the wall fell to the ground. Heads appeared from out of the doors all along the corridor. Jones grabbed a fistful of Walker's shirt, twisted it and lifted him onto his toes then leaned forward and hissed into this ear, 'Your little girlfriend has had it this time.' He gave Walker a shove causing him to totter but he saved himself from falling by grabbing the doorjamb.

'I've had worse than that from a copper before, Jones, you bloody goon.'

'Say one more thing and I'll arrest you too, Walker. Obstructing a police officer performing his duty.'

Walker jerked his shirtfront down and straightened his tie, scowling at Jones, but remained silent.

Jones turned back to Angela, who was standing unsteadily, the female police officer holding her firmly by the upper arm. 'Now, you can come with us, girlie. Or are you going to cause trouble like your boyfriend?'

Angela shook her head. Jones snapped at the policewoman. 'Get on with it.'

Moments later she was led away.

Walker watched them go, feeling helpless. He called out after them, 'I'll call Cassandra, Angela.'

But before she could answer the trio had turned a corner and were gone.

Darling was already in the interview room of the Parramatta police station when Angela was led in by Jones and the female officer. A moment later Cassandra Hollows turned up closely followed by Walker, red-faced with exertion.

'Not this time, Kit," Darling said. 'This is an arrest.'

'Yes, this time,' countered Cassandra. 'You know as well as I do that a suspect is allowed a friend present during the interview.'

Darling grunted but said nothing. Walker took a chair in the corner and rested his hands on his lap. Angela and Cassandra sat opposite Darling and Jones took a chair beside his superior, rocking on the edge like an excited hound.

'Dr Chee,' Darling began, 'I understand Senior Constable Jones has told you your rights. Do you want me to go over them again?'

Angela shook her head.

'Get on with it, Barry,' said Cassandra. 'What's this all about?'

Darling flicked a hand at Jones who sat even further upright before speaking. 'Dr Chee, we have security camera footage showing you throwing a bag into a waste bin in the rear dock of the hospital on the same day your father was murdered.'

'So?' said Cassandra. 'You can't arrest someone for being tidy.'

Jones gave a triumphant smile. 'We managed to get to the bin before it was collected.' He threw a clear plastic bag onto the desktop. It had a distinctive orange band printed on it and inside several medicine vials could be seen.

Cassandra leaned forward to read the label. 'Metoprolol.'

'Exactly,' said Jones with finality in his voice.

There was silence. Angela stared at her lap while the others in the room stared at her.

'Can you explain this?' Darling asked softly.

Angela shook her head but still said nothing.

'Do you deny that you threw the bag containing metoprolol into the bin?'

The young doctor failed to raise her eyes.

'It is definitely you in the footage. And the plastic bag with an orange stripe can be clearly seen.'

When Angela didn't speak, Darling started up again. 'Angela Chee, we are charging you with the murder of Benjamin Chee. Do you understand what I'm saying?'

Angela nodded but kept her eyes fixed on her lap.

'You will be remanded in custody for the moment.'

Darling turned to Cassandra, who sat stiff-faced, not looking at her client. 'Ms Hollow, you know murder has an automatic presumption against bail. But in this case, the police will support an application for bail. She's low risk.'

'I should be able to get a hearing from a magistrate tomorrow morning, first thing,' said Cassandra. Finally, she looked at Angela. 'Don't worry, Angie, you have a good chance of having bail granted. The magistrate should agree with Detective Darling's assessment that you are low risk for reoffending. It's common for bail to be granted in such a situation.'

Jones stood and indicated that Angela should do the same with a jerk of his thumb. 'But for now, we'll find a nice cosy cell for you to relax in.'

Angela stood with her head down, her gaze locked onto the floor before her. Jones waved towards the door and the female constable came in, took Angela's arm and steered her towards the door.

As she turned, Angela finally raised her head. Her eyes locked onto Walker's.

He opened his mouth to talk but realised he had nothing to say. Angela was led out of the room.

Walker and Cassandra met at the Epping pub that evening and sat together at a high table in a corner away from the bar. Cassandra wore a tight white dress cut low at the front and high at the hem, which attracted a lot of looks from men and women alike. But she was oblivious to the stares and gazed glumly down into her beer, drawing circles with a red fingernail on the tabletop.

'Do you think she really did it?' she asked.

'I don't know,' said Walker. 'I don't want to believe it.'

'You can't blame her after what her father did to her mother.'

'But she doesn't seem the type.'

'The type to murder?' Cassandra looked up. 'And what type is that? Any of us could commit murder in the right – or should I say wrong – circumstances. I see that often enough in my line of business.'

'I just can't believe she would do it,' Walker repeated.

'But what about the drug?'

He grimaced. 'Looks suspicious. I can't think of any reason why she would have ampoules of metoprolol, let alone throw them out into a general waste bin in the dead of night.'

'So you think she did it?'

'I didn't say that.'

'But you're thinking it.'

'What about you?'

Cassandra sighed. 'I don't know what to think. She didn't deny she threw the drugs away. And it was the same drug that killed her father. What else can we believe?'

Walker shook his head glumly. 'Don't know.'

'But we also have the murder of the pharmacist," said Cassandra. 'I very much doubt that Angela can drive a forklift.'

She looked around the bar and leaned forward towards Walker, her mouth close to his ear. 'Anyway, with Angela locked up I'll be all alone in the apartment tonight.' She took another long sip of her glass and eyed Walker over the rim.

Walker twisted on his stool uncomfortably. 'Will you be okay?' he asked, although he was fairly certain she wasn't frightened of being alone.

Instead of answering his question, she swivelled sideways in her chair. On the table next to her bag was a glossy magazine with a model posing in a skimpy blue bikini. She leaned back on her stool, stretched her long, tanned legs and discreetly edged the hem of her skirt up on the side closest to Walker. She tapped the photo of the model's legs and then raised her eyebrows. 'What do you think?'

Walker cleared his throat and glanced around uncomfortably. They were in a dark corner of the pub and no one was looking. 'Very nice.' His voice was strained.

'Mine or hers?'

'Both.'

She glanced around the pub then back at Walker. 'Have you ever wanted to stroke them?'

Walker looked at the photo and then down at Cassandra's long legs, stretched out invitingly.

She bit her lip as she ran her fingertip up the inside of her leg and she raised her eyebrows. 'Mmm?' Her voice became husky as her hand gently moved higher. She looked at him, her eyes wide. 'Do you?'

Walker's voice was not much more than a whisper. 'What about Barry?'

'Oh, I don't really want both of you tonight. One at a time will do.'

Walker took a deep breath and let it out slowly.

He looked down at her long legs and reached out his hand.

# CHAPTER NINETEEN

BLUE AND WHITE chequered tape roped off a corner of the area outside the main lecture theatre at Western Meadow Hospital and Walker stood behind it, peering in at the small crowd that had gathered. Barry Darling and Constable Jones were there along with a few other plain-clothed officers who were taking photos, dusting for prints and measuring with a cloth tape.

Walker had a headache. He had gone home by himself the night before and had had a restless sleep.

Darling saw Walker and approached him but stayed on the other side of the tape. 'Another murder. Or at least it might be. No obvious injuries, but there is a needle mark in his left forearm.' He looked down at his notepad. 'Andrzej Korbmann, a wardsman.' He looked up again. 'Isn't he the one who was involved with Chee and the Masons?'

'Andy? You're kidding. Who'd want to kill him? He wouldn't hurt a fly.'

'Saw something he shouldn't have, maybe? Who knows?'

'This is unbelievable,' said Walker. 'What's going on around here? Another murder?' He stared at the body that was slumped against the wall in a dark corner of the crush area, with various people buzzing around, brushing and prodding, taking photos, as if he were an actor being prepared for a show. 'No injury, you say. You think it's poison?'

'Or he could have had a heart attack. We won't know until the autopsy and forensics.'

'If Andy was murdered at least we know that wasn't Angela. You've got her locked up.'

Darling grunted. 'We'll see what the drug lab says about his blood. They already have a sample and I've asked them to fast-track it, looking for metoprolol. Should have an answer by tomorrow. We'll move the body down to the morgue and make sure he didn't die of natural causes.' He turned back to Walker and drew his lips into a smile but his eyes remained sober. 'Handy having the coroner on-site with all these murders. Autopsies-while-you-wait. Wish it was always that easy.' He looked back at the body again. 'Where did he work?'

'Andy? All over, I suppose. Not sure how the wardsmen are rostered. But he was in our cancer ward a lot. Been here for ages. Everyone knows him. Polish. Jewish, I think. Came out with his parents after the war. Cheerful and helpful. Everyone liked him.'

'You seem to know a lot about him.'

Walker shrugged. 'I've worked with him for years. When I was a registrar doing twenty-four-hour shifts, you got to know everyone. Forced together in a hospital all weekend. We all had dinner together in the cafeteria. We weren't friends though.'

Walker moved closer and dropped his voice. 'Wendy, what do you think is going on around here? Three people dead. Do you think they're related, or is it just some lunatic killing at random?'

'We don't know yet. We don't even know if Andy was murdered. Do you know where his supervisor would be?'

'The wardsmen have an area on the bottom floor in the basement at the opposite end of the hospital.' He pointed. 'Walk up that corridor until you're almost to the end, take a right and then take the stairs down one flight. You'll see it as you come out of the stairs.'

Darling moved away in the direction Walker had pointed.

'Wendy,' called Walker and he stopped. 'Are you seeing Cassandra Hollows? Dating her, I mean?'

Darling turned fully. 'What's it to you? You interested in her?'

Walker paused before replying. 'No, but she's Angela's best friend. And her lawyer. Not sure it's right you two going out together, being on other sides of a case. Is that against the law?'

Darling visibly stiffened. 'Mind your own business, Kit. No, it is *not* against the law. You have no right sticking your nose into my love-life. Sort your own out before you start dishing out advice.' Darling gritted his teeth. 'Does Angela know what you did to Flea? No? Well, maybe I'll tell her. Do her a favour.' He half-turned to go but stopped again. 'Just keep your nose out of my business.'

Walker watched wordlessly as Darling walked away, a sober look on his face.

Later that morning, Darling sought out Walker in his office and asked him to accompany him to the pharmacy. Maisie Diver, the director of pharmacy, had called Darling that morning. She had information, she said, about the murder cases.

They moved along a grubby service corridor littered with broken beds and IV poles until they reached the pharmacy. Walker was able to use his pass to enter the first doors that opened into a small cubicle with thick glass doors on the opposite side. Walker knew his pass wouldn't work on those; only pharmacists were authorised to enter. A secretary greeted them and a few minutes later, Maisie Diver stood at the open glass door, wearing a loose-fitting dress.

'Sorry about the casual clothes,' she said over her shoulder as they entered her office. 'This hot weather's a killer. Especially down here. It gets so muggy and the air conditioning often doesn't work.'

She turned as she reached her desk. 'I've identified the glass ampoule you gave me.' She held up the plastic bag that contained the stub of the ampoule with a yellow band around it.

'Great,' said Walker. 'What is it? Metoprolol?'

'No,' she said with a curious expression. 'Pancuronium.'

'Pancuronium!' said Walker. 'Wow.'

'What's pan cure ...' asked Darling, stumbling over the word.

'Pancuronium,' repeated Walker. 'It's a muscle relaxant. Like curare. They use it in anaesthetics.'

'Curare,' said Darling. 'You mean like the pygmies with blowpipes? Poison?'

'Exactly,' said Walker.

'Except,' Maisie corrected, 'curare's used by the natives in South America, not the pygmies of Africa. And they mostly use it on arrows.'

Walker shrugged. 'Same thing.'

Maisie made a face.

'Anyway,' continued Walker, 'the end result is the same. It paralyses the muscles so you can't move and you stop breathing.'

'Curare or pancudodium?' asked Darling.

'Pan-cure-onium,' Maisie said helpfully.

'Both,' said Walker. 'They do the same thing.' He raised his eyebrows at Maisie. 'I think.'

'Yes, we don't use curare anymore. Pancuronium is a synthetic version and shorter acting. It's used to relax the muscles during an anaesthetic so it is easier to ventilate the patient.'

'But importantly,' added Walker, 'you don't lose consciousness. You have perfect use of your faculties. They always use a sedative before it, otherwise the person just lays there, unable to move a muscle, unable to speak or breathe.' He shivered visibly. 'What an awful way to go.'

Darling held up the plastic bag containing the ampoule and addressed Maisie. 'Are you sure?'

'Positive.'

She pointed to an unbroken ampoule on her desk, which Darling picked up, and Walker and he examined it closely. The full ampoule was about five centimetres high and had a white label with 'pancuronium' written in red, and other text below in black. Around the neck of the ampoule was a yellow band that looked exactly like the stub in the plastic bag.

'The shape of the stub and the colour and size of the band matches exactly,' Maisie added.

'I agree,' said Darling. He looked up. 'Who else knows about this?'

'No one,' she said. 'With what happened to Sanjeev, I've told no one. I've done the searching myself.'

'Good,' said Darling. 'The next job is to find where the murderer got it from. Are there any reports of ampoules missing?'

'We'll have to do a stocktake.'

'Can I suggest you start in the endoscopy unit?' said Walker. 'That's where Sanjeev was working before he was killed.'

'Good idea,' agreed Darling. 'How long will that take?'

'Just the endoscopy unit?' said Maisie. 'I can do that by this afternoon.'

'Excellent,' said Darling. 'Great work, Maisie,' he added with a broad smile. 'You've helped enormously.'

Maisie leaned forward and opened the bottom drawer of her desk to place the unbroken pancuronium ampoule into it, causing her shift to billow open. She looked up and flashed a smile. 'It's been my pleasure.'

Darling's smile broadened. 'Well, maybe I'll think of some way to thank you more appropriately.'

As Maisie stood her smile matched his. She offered her hand for him to shake. 'Looking forward to it.'

After Maisie had seen them out and they were walking again along the empty service corridor, Walker grumbled to Darling, 'Thought you were seeing Cassie.'

Darling bristled but then had a change of heart. He smiled. 'Cassie. Maisie.' He waved his arms magnanimously. 'Both beautiful women, there's no doubting that. When you're young and single like me, Kit, the world is your oyster.'

'I'm single too,' Walker grunted.

'You,' Darling huffed, his smile fading. 'You've become an old man. You don't know how to have fun anymore.' Now he frowned. 'Something to do with Flea, perhaps?'

'It's nothing to do with Flea,' snapped Walker.

Darling stopped and put a hand on his arm, pulling him up. 'You'll have to tell me about Flea one day.'

'Why? It's nothing to do with you.'

Darling was silent for a moment, mulling a thought over in his mind. Then he said slowly, 'I've spoken to Sergeant Kora from Mount Hagen police.'

Walker seemed momentarily shocked. His lips tightened and he looked out into the garden courtyard, speechless. Darling thought he looked nervous.

'Why would you do that?' asked Walker.

'I don't think we have the full story about Flea. There's something missing. There is something not right. Your reaction, for starters. You know there is more to tell. You may have been able to fool the coppers in New Guinea but you can't fool me. I know when someone's lying. Especially you.'

'I'm not lying.' Walker was blank-faced. Then he got a faraway look. 'It's just that I don't remember everything that happened.' He frowned but still seemed to be elsewhere. 'I almost drowned. I was out of it.' Now he looked at Darling. He licked his lips. 'I get these dreams. That I'm trying to save her. Under the water. But she pushes herself away from me.' He looked away again. 'And other dreams.'

'What dreams?'

Walker came back to the present and flashed a frown at Darling. 'Can't say. Can't remember. They're not clear.'

'About Felicity?'

He nodded, his face stiff.

'Something to do with her death?'

'No.' He looked down at the ground and spoke softly. 'After her death.'

'About Felicity *after* her death? With her body? What do you mean?'

'Can't say,' repeated Walker. He seemed to be elsewhere again. 'Can't remember.' When he looked at Darling, his face had cleared and he shook his head briskly. 'All rubbish. They're nothing. They can't be true.'

'What?' Darling insisted.

But Walker just shook his head again and started walking along the corridor. 'Come on, Wendy,' he called back. 'You've got a murder to solve.'


Walker agreed to meet Angela that night at the Orient Hotel in The Rocks. She'd phoned him at his office that afternoon after she had been released on bail. She had news for him, she said.

The Orient was one of the few colonial buildings that had been continuously used as a pub and one of the oldest in Australia and a popular music venue on weekends. But on this Wednesday night, the jukebox was playing and Brian Adams' sultry voice oozed out from the speakers above their heads.

Walker noticed that Angela silently mouthed the words and he made a quick mental note. He wasn't a particular fan but he could at least tolerate Adams' music.

They sat at a table away from the bar so they could speak and eat a quick snack of noodles from the kitchen. Walker had a schooner of VB in front of him while Angela sipped on a glass of the house chardonnay.

'Are you okay at home?' he asked.

'They won't let me go back to work. The clinical super's office said so. At least until the charges have been dropped.'

Walker thought she sounded confident. 'Will they be?'

She stopped eating and looked at him. 'I didn't do it.'

'Of course not,' he said quickly. He wanted to ask her about the bag of drugs she'd been caught throwing out. Instead he asked, 'What will you do while you're waiting?'

She shrugged. 'It's my father's funeral in a few days. They've finally released the body. So there's that to attend to. Otherwise, I don't feel like doing anything. I'm completely shattered.'

'Have you heard about Andy?' he asked.

'Terrible.' Then she shook her head sadly. 'Who would do that? What is happening at the hospital? Why are so many people dying?'

Walker felt a stab of guilt. His initial impulse was to distrust her. He didn't know why since there was no way she could have killed Andy. Her alibi was rock solid. She'd been in a police cell at the time.

But the business with her discarding the metoprolol was still not explained. Could she have killed her father? Walker couldn't forget her strange reaction to his death, how she refused to help resuscitate him. It was her father after all. She should have tried. He would have if it was his father. And what possible explanation did she have for having the drug? He again resisted the temptation to ask her outright. He knew there was no way of verifying whatever answer she gave without sounding suspicious. As much as he hated to admit it, he'd have to leave it to Wendy to sort out.

She took a sip of her wine then rubbed her hands together and looked around the room.

When she looked back, she spoke rapidly. 'I can't help feeling that Professor McBrent had something to do with my father's death.'

Walker didn't immediately answer. 'Why do you say that?' he finally asked. Why say it now?

'I don't think he liked my father.' Her normally smooth brow was knitted together and she continued quickly. 'I think there was something with my mother. I think he loved her.'

'McBrent? And your mother?' Walker had the impression that her emotions were all wrong. She should have been angry, but instead she seemed nervous.

'He could have got hold of metoprolol as easy as anything.' She took a deep breath and huffed it out. 'Why are they trying to blame my father's death on me? Anyone could have got a few ampoules. Even Andy. Why, I saw Sandy going through the arrest trolley on the ward. Gloria and him. Said he was checking what was in it. Anyone could have taken it.'

He wanted to say *But none of them had been caught throwing out a bag of metoprolol*, but instead he said, 'So who was it then? McBrent, Andy, Sandy or Gloria?'

She looked away again and shook her head. 'Anyone.' She took another sip of her wine and looked out of the window onto George Street, deep in thought.

Where she turned back, she seemed resigned and calmer. 'I don't know, Chris. I just don't know why the police are picking on me.'

The music changed and another slow ballad started up.

Walker's head dropped theatrically and he pretended to dry retch.

Angela gave him a bemused smile. 'You don't like Michael Bolton?'

'It's terrible,' he moaned. He began crooning along with the song – 'How Am I Supposed to Live Without You' – exaggerating Bolton's sentimental tones. Then he picked up the chopsticks he'd used to eat his dinner. 'If I have to listen to this soppy rubbish another time, I'll be forced to poke these through my eardrums.'

Angela laughed, a delicate tinkle, her previous agitation dissolved. 'Well, in that case, let's go outside and get some fresh air.'

Carrying their glasses, they walked out to the back of the pub where the courtyard was filled with drinkers, despite it being a Wednesday night. They managed to find a quiet spot in a corner.

'Professor McBrent came to my apartment today,' she said as soon as she was seated.

'What for?'

'He was after the photos.'

'Did he say that? Did he mention photos or was he still pretending he was after a paper your father had written?'

'At first he did, but when he realised I didn't believe him he came out with it. He said he didn't want the photos to get out. Didn't want the publicity to sully my mother's memory. But it was obvious what his real intention was.'

Walker paused thoughtfully. He wondered whether Angela knew that it was he who had given the photos to Darling. 'What did you say?' he asked finally.

'I said I knew nothing about them.'

Walker grunted. 'Good.'

'But, Chris, we know the police have them. They found them when they searched my father's house.'

Walker didn't want to tell her that it had been he who had given them to Darling. 'Had you seen them?'

Angela went silent and she dropped her head. 'Yes, once. When I was in my final year of school. My father and mother were out and I went into my father's office looking for a pen. The cabinet was open and I saw the photos. Only a few of them. I was shocked. I couldn't believe my mother would do that.' She looked up and there were tears in her eyes. 'She looked as if she liked it. I didn't know what to do. What to think. It's for that reason – that look of ecstasy on her face, the total enjoyment – that I did not denounce my father. But I still hated him for it. He should have loved her, cared for her. He should not have let other men do that to her, even if she wanted it.' She rubbed one hand over the other. 'I've been so confused all these years.'

She went silent again and stared at the tabletop, allowing her fingers to intertwine each other like small snakes. When she looked up there was defiance on her face. 'But I tell you one thing. I'm glad he's dead.'

Just at the wrong moment, the music changed to the Divinyls, the rising crescendo of a bass guitar like blood pumping in a skull followed by the raw sexuality of Chrissy Amphlett's voice singing 'I touch myself'.

In Walker's mind, it was the most inappropriate song imaginable at this point in their conversation. He couldn't stop visualising the photos of Lucia Chee, her mouth open and head thrown back at the point of orgasm. And sitting right in front of him was her daughter, so much like her mother, at least in appearance. He wondered whether Angela was imagining the same thing.

The fact that Walker had a crush on Chrissy Amphlett didn't make him feel any better. He couldn't stop his thoughts. Was Angela like her mother? Would she love sex as much as her mother seemed to? He let out a deep breath and looked away. He had to stop thinking of those things right now while Angela was so vulnerable. When he looked up, she was staring at him as if she could read his mind.

'I feel really strange,' she said.

She looked at a group of revellers who were drinking nearby. A girl in a tight red dress was kissing a young man, standing between his legs as he sat on a stool, his hands slowly moving down her back to caress her buttocks.

Angela looked back at Walker. 'Do you want to go?' she asked quietly.

'Where?'

'Your place?' Her voice was hoarse.

They walked quickly out the back gate of the courtyard into a lane and then onto Argyle Street. Angela held his arm close against her chest, her arm wrapped tightly around his. Their hips pushed against each other and Walker had to shorten his step so they could walk in unison. He slipped his arm out of her grip and put his hand on her other hip to steady her and he felt her muscles ripple beneath his palm.

Angela said nothing. He could feel her puffing as they made their way up the slope, her breast hard against his chest. They reached his terrace and he fumbled with the keys while she still held him tightly. Archie the cat looked at them lazily from the corner of the veranda with half-closed eyes.

As soon as they were through, she was on him, pushing him hard against the closed door, her arms tight around his neck, pulling his mouth onto hers.

She stepped away, reached behind, and unzipped her dress.

# CHAPTER TWENTY

WALKER WAS WOKEN early in the morning by a call, the shrill bell of the phone wrenching him out of the deep sleep he'd finally fallen into only a few hours before he was due to arise.

Before that, his sleep had been fitful but at least he couldn't remember dreaming about Flea. But the bedcovers were tangled around as if he had wrestled all night and his pillow was on the ground.

Then he remembered.

Angela!

He raised his head and looked around the room.

She was gone.

He rubbed his face roughly, trying to kick his mind into action while the phone continued to scream at him from the bedside table. His lids were thick and his eyes ached. He was sure they'd be bloodshot, but he couldn't even get the damned things to open!

Finally, he fumbled the receiver off the cradle, pushed it against his tender scalp and grunted into it.

'You still asleep, Kit? I thought you medicos started early.'

'Bugger off, Wendy, I'm not a bloody surgeon.' Walker rubbed his eyes with stiff fingers. 'What do you want?'

'The lab results have come back on both Andy Korbmann and Benjamin Chee,' Darling paused. 'Pancuronium in both of them. Lots of it.'

'They're both dead, Wendy, you bloody turd. What's the urgency? Why call me now?'

'I'll meet you at the hospital,' he barked, then the phone went dead.

An hour later and still feeling woolly-headed, Walker met Darling outside the lecture theatres, which were empty at that time of day. Darling looked annoyingly chipper and he thrust a takeaway coffee cup into his hands and beckoned him away from the main thoroughfare.

'Did Korbmann have metoprolol in his blood as well?' asked Walker, taking a gulp of the coffee. Then he looked into the cup and moaned. 'Did you get this from the hospital? Don't you know it's rubbish?'

Darling ignored that. 'No, just the pancuronium in Korbmann's blood.'

Walker threw the coffee into a nearby bin. 'And have you found out where it came from?'

'Maisie Diver said a box of ten ampoules is missing from the endoscopy suite. That's what Sanjeev must have discovered before he was killed.'

Walker rubbed his face then jerked his head up. 'So that proves Angela didn't kill her father.'

'Not at all. She obviously didn't kill Korbmann because she was in custody. But she could have killed her father. She still hasn't said what she was doing with the metoprolol and why she threw it away. And there was also metoprolol in her father's blood, enough to kill him.'

'But to have that stack up, there'd have to be two killers: Angela to kill Chee and then another for Korbmann. And who drove into Sanjeev with a forklift?'

Darling eyed Walker. 'Is it a coincidence that it was you two who discovered her father's body?'

He said nothing for a moment while Darling's comment sunk in. Then he exploded. 'Are you serious, Wendy? You can't honestly believe I had anything to do with it?'

'Why not? You could've easily knocked him off. And you could have done in Korbmann to prove your girlfriend didn't do it. And who found Sanjeev dead? You. I reckon you could drive a forklift.'

'Girlfriend?' Walker couldn't block the images of Angela out of his mind. Or were they the images of her mother? Like the photos. He couldn't shake the feeling that Angela had another reason to sleep with him.

Why had he done it? Why had she done it? Why now? Why like that? Like her mother?

Walker mind skated from one thought to the other, desperately trying to think of something else.

He pushed a finger into Darling's chest. 'Speaking of girlfriends, guess who I was with the night that Korbmann was murdered?' Walker stepped away with a triumphant look on his face. 'Cassandra Hollow.'

Darling looked stunned. 'Cassie? What do you mean? You were with her? Bullshit! She wouldn't touch you with a barge pole.'

'Oh yeah? That's what you think. She's a real goer, you know. Cassie's very open. Very sexually liberated. And she's got smashing thighs. Smooth as silk.'

Darling let fly a quick right hook that caught Walker in the side of the head, causing him to stumble backwards, but he managed to lean away from the left uppercut he knew would follow. He kicked Darling between the legs and as he doubled over in pain, Walker grabbed both shoulders and shoved him backwards into the table behind. But Darling managed to hang onto Walker's left arm and pulled him down to the ground with him. They wrestled in a tight hug, punching each other in the chest and face when they could get a fist free.

A moment later they were pulled apart and sat gasping, staring at each other, Jones looming over both, keeping them apart with a beefy hand on each shoulder. Jones moved behind Walker and grabbed him under the arms, dragging him to his feet.

'You're under arrest, sunshine. Assaulting a police officer should do you nicely.'

'Let him go.' Darling coughed, his voice hoarse. Blood was oozing out of one nostril and his top lip was split.

'Let him go? Are you kidding, boss? I saw him attack you.'

'I attacked him.' Darling held a handkerchief to his nose. 'He was just protecting himself.'

Jones was clearly unhappy. 'Well then, he was resisting arrest.'

'I wasn't arresting him.' He pointed his bloodied handkerchief at Walker. 'He hasn't got the balls to murder anyone.'

Walker had a cut above his left eyebrow and blood was streaming down the side of his face into his eye, the lid already swollen and starting to close over.

Darling reached into his pocket, pulled out another handkerchief and thrust it at Walker. After a moment's hesitation he accepted it, pushing it firmly against the gash.

'Where does that leave us then?' he asked. 'You don't think I killed Korbmann and neither did Angela.'

'It was a doctor,' Darling said doggedly. 'Or someone with access to drugs.'

'What about a nurse?' said Walker. He raised his chin defiantly. 'What about Maisie Diver?'

Darling frowned and gave his nose another pat. 'Don't be a dickhead. Maisie's got nothing to do with it.'

'My point is it could be almost anyone in the hospital.'

'But not everyone had a motive to kill Chee. And not everyone had the opportunity to access pancuronium. From what Maisie says, it's only stored in the pharmacy, the anaesthetic areas of the operating suite and endoscopy, and they're all accessed by pass cards.' He shook his head. 'No, it's got to be someone with access *and* a motive, at least to kill Chee. Sanjeev and the wardsman might be collateral damage.'

Darling waved to Jones. 'Track down Professor McBrent. I think we should have another talk with him.'

Jones gave Walker a final scowl then stormed off towards McBrent's office. But then he stopped and turned back. 'Sir, I came to tell you that the Singaporean police are trying to get hold of you. They want you to call them back.'

'Thanks, Jones,' said Darling. 'I'll deal with that shortly.'

After Jones had left, Darling patted his lip then looked at Walker. 'Did you sleep with Cassandra? Tell me the truth.'

Walker pulled the cloth away from his gash and studied the blood before he spoke. 'No. No, I did not. Apparently, she likes *you*. For the life of me, I don't know why.'

'So you tried it then, is that it?'

He shook his head. 'No, I didn't.' He pressed the cloth back onto his face. 'She's not my type.' He didn't want to tell him how she'd flirted outrageously with him in the pub. More than flirt.

Darling straightened his tie and shirt and buckled his belt, which had come loose in the fracas. 'Okay then.' He seemed relieved but Walker thought he was trying to hide it. 'Sorry for punching you in the head.'

Walker let out a short laugh. 'You're not sorry. You've been wanting to do that for years.'

Darling curled up his mouth thoughtfully. 'Yeah, I guess I have.' He didn't look happy. 'Somehow it doesn't make me feel any better though.'

Walker rubbed his face, careful not to touch the laceration. 'Where does that leave us?'

Darling shrugged and looked at the ground. 'Don't know. I don't think I'll know how I feel about you until the truth about Flea comes out.' He raised his eyes questioningly.

But Walker dropped his head and moved slowly away.


Darling and Constable Jones found McBrent in his office, a long, narrow room off one of the corridors in the clinical building. The walls were adorned with academic degrees in frames and an oil painting of McBrent sitting in a red armchair, his face turned away but his eyes wide, looking sideways at the artist as if he'd been caught in the middle of something. The orange of his hair was exaggerated and the skin of his face looked red and worn. Darling thought the portrait was far from flattering but probably appropriate. Perhaps the artist, whoever it was, knew more about his subject than McBrent realised.

McBrent sat at his desk and swivelled towards them. He stared from face to face expectantly.

'Professor McBrent, we'd like to ask you a few more questions, if that's all right,' Darling began.

He appeared annoyed. 'I'm busy. I *am* the Professor of Medicine, you know.' He gestured to a stack of papers on the desk behind him. A computer sat beside the pile but the screen was off. 'I've told you everything I know about CCU.' Then he put on an exaggeratedly resigned expression. 'What do you want to know?'

'It's not about the CCU, professor. We now know that Professor Chee was also injected with,' he read from his notebook, 'pancuronium.'

McBrent made a face. 'Ooh. That's pretty nasty. Not a nice way to die. But what has that got to do with me?'

'And two nights ago, a wardsman was also murdered with the same drug.'

Darling watched his expression carefully but the professor remained unconcerned. 'Shouldn't you be out trying to catch the killer? What if more people are murdered?' Then his expression changed abruptly. 'Oh no! You think the killer might be after me?' He stood up stiffly. 'But this is terrible. You need to protect me. He must be stopped.'

'Relax, professor,' said Jones. 'We don't think you're a target.'

'But how do you know?' McBrent continued, agitated. 'You don't even know why the murders are happening. Whoever it is might be after me.'

'And why would that be?' asked Darling.

'Because I'm the *professor*.' He punched his chest with his fist repeatedly. 'I'm the most important person around here.'

'Is there a more specific reason that someone might want you dead?'

'What do you mean?' Now he looked suspicious.

Darling gestured to Jones who handed McBrent a folder. He opened it and stared down at the contents – copies of the photos of himself with Lucia Chee. He looked up, wide-eyed. 'Where did you get these? Did that little bitch Angela Chee give them to you?'

'Never mind that, professor. I think it's time you told us about your relationship with Benjamin Chee and his wife.'

McBrent examined the photos then snapped the folder shut and he calmed noticeably. 'I didn't break any laws.' His voice had become steady. 'Chee and his wife were both consenting. Lucia enjoyed it. And so did Chee.' He raised his eyebrows. 'And so did I, for that matter. Lucia Chee was a beautiful woman. And she really liked sex. I mean *really*.' He made a fist with both hands and shook them. 'But Benjamin and I had a bit of a falling out.'

'What about?'

McBrent's manner changed and he rotated his head as if his neck was causing discomfort. 'It was nothing about Lucia. Well, not directly at least. Chee was trying to join a club that I belong to. But somehow our ... activities were discovered.' His eyes flicked from one man to the other before he continued. 'The ... ah, club ... didn't want to have anything to do with him. Chee was furious, and he blamed me for it. But I didn't tell anyone. Why would I? I was implicated too. Thank God, they didn't find out about me. I prayed to Jesus they didn't and He answered my prayers. Nothing came of it. Except they rejected Chee, of course.' He smiled.

Jones glanced at Darling before speaking to McBrent. 'You prayed to Jesus that no one would find out that you were having sex with your friend's wife while he took photos?'

McBrent's face remained thoughtful. 'Exactly. And Jesus answered my prayers.'

Darling cleared his throat and looked down at his notes then looked up. 'Did this ... club happen to be the Freemasons?'

McBrent looked surprised. 'Yes, it was. How did you know?'

'And was Andy Korbmann also involved?'

Again, McBrent looked surprised. 'You have excellent information. How did you find that out? No one knew, as far as I could tell.'

Darling noted that he looked interested rather than anxious. 'So, you and Andy Korbmann were sponsoring Benjamin Chee's entry into the Masons?'

'That's right.'

'And what is your relationship with Korbmann?'

McBrent shrugged. 'He works in the hospital. And we are both members of the same Masonic chapter.'

'Did Korbmann have anything to do with Professor Chee and his wife?'

McBrent smirked. 'I doubt it. I doubt very much that Benjamin would allow a wardsman to do *that* to his wife. I knew what Chee was after.'

'And what's that?'

'He was after promotion. He only involved those at the hospital and university who could pave the way for him, so to speak. A hospital wardsman couldn't do that.'

'Korbmann was sponsoring him for the Masons. Maybe he was grateful?'

McBrent shook his head. 'I doubt it. I can't see Lucia with a man like Korbmann. She liked doctors and professors. Men of power and influence. It turned her on.'

Darling stared at McBrent for a few moments then looked down at his notes. Without looking up, he said, 'Did you ever see Lucia without Chee?' Now he held McBrent's eyes in a steely gaze. 'Did you develop a relationship with Lucia Chee that was more than sexual? And did Benjamin Chee find out?'

'Certainly not.'

Darling persisted. 'Did he threaten to tell your wife? Did you have to shut him up?'

'No! No way.' McBrent was finally ruffled. 'Our relationship was all above board. All legal. It was a transaction – three-way. Benjamin, Lucia and I all got something out of it. There was no love or emotion involved from my point of view. Sex only.'

'Did Lucia fall in love with you, perhaps?' Darling noticed the look of disbelief on Jones' face. He felt the same but he had to follow the line of inquiry. 'Did she fall in love with you, and Chee became jealous? Was he making things difficult for you at work?'

'No!' McBrent gasped. 'Anyway, why would I kill him now? That was five years ago. Lucia is long gone.'

Darling looked down at his pad again and made a note. 'Where were you the night before last?'

'The night before last? I was with my wife. We were at a function at the Art Gallery in the city. An opening of aboriginal art.'

'And afterwards?'

'I went home.'

'Did you come back to the hospital?' asked Jones.

'Certainly not. Why would I?'

Jones paused in thought before speaking. 'Was Korbmann at the opening earlier that evening?'

McBrent became irritated. 'Korbmann? No! I don't know. What would a wardsman be doing at a premier social event? Why all these questions about Korbmann? Ask him yourself!'

'So, a wardsman can't like art?' persisted Jones.

'Of course he can,' snapped McBrent. 'But he wouldn't be invited to an opening. I don't even like the bloody stuff. All dots and squiggles. But my wife is a member and we needed to go. She needs to be seen.'

'Do you mind if we check with your wife?'

Now McBrent became agitated. 'What for? Ask someone else. I'll give you a list of names. I don't want my wife getting mixed up in any of this.' He held up the folder. 'She certainly does not need to know anything about this.'

'We need to know where you were after the gallery opening,' said Jones. 'Were you with anyone else that night, apart from your wife?'

Both Darling and Jones waited with undisguised interest for McBrent's answer.

Finally, he shook his head. 'No. No, only my wife.'

'Then we will have to interview her,' Jones said with satisfaction.

'Go ahead,' said McBrent with a resigned look. Then he held up the folder of photos again. 'But if you mention anything about this, I'll have your job.'


Walker had considered going home. His head ached from where Darling had punched him. The laceration over his eye stung and from the evidence on the pad when he pulled it away, the cut still oozed blood. But, reluctantly, he made his way up to the ward.

He had to do a ward round. He owed it to his patients.

It wasn't that he didn't trust his team but they weren't as experienced as he was.

He let out a sigh. No, it was true. He really didn't trust them. His intern was an idiot, and the medical student was just that – a student. And Angela was still off work and, with all the events of the last weeks, he just couldn't trust her.

He took the elevator rather the stairs and reached the ward, feeling sorry for himself. But Jenny, as pretty as ever in her tight nurse's uniform, made a satisfactory fuss when she saw him and he began to feel better.

'Christopher, you're bleeding! What happened? Come, sit here, I'll dress it.'

He sat on a chair in the middle of the nurses' station while several nurses bustled around, pulling out dressing packs and bandages. One of the nurses called him a naughty boy for fighting and another one said he deserved a smack, while others tittered and chortled behind Jenny as she started work on him.

He was conscious of Jenny's nimble fingers on his scalp as she cleaned off the blood. She wanted him to rest his head against her chest to keep it still and he could feel her small breasts through her thin uniform. Finally, she pulled the gash together with Steri-Strips and placed a dressing to cover her handiwork, then gave him a light kiss on his forehead.

With her hands on his shoulders, she bent close to his ear and whispered, 'Look after yourself, Christopher Walker,' then moved away, leaving him by himself on the chair. Beforehand, he'd felt a sexual thrill from her body contact but with her words, he now felt sad. Alone.

He looked around. All the nurses had gone back to their tasks, their fun over.

Gloria stood nearby, leaning on the nurses' bench, an uncharacteristically thoughtful look on her face. She remained silent as she examined him, unsmiling.

He rose awkwardly, feeling embarrassed. 'We should get on with the round.'

Gloria looked down at the file in her hands, her lips pulled down. 'Mr Aaron Young's brain CT is clear. There's nothing that would explain his fits.'

Walker got the distinct impression of an air of superiority from her, as if somehow he'd been shown to be weak and now the CT report confirmed it.

'I said it would be normal,' he snapped.

She pulled her lips down even further. 'What's causing it then?' She made it sound like a challenge.

Walker felt like swearing but stopped himself. Instead, he walked towards her and she stood upright with a startled look, as if realising she'd overstepped.

'Show me the EEG report.' He hoped she didn't have it so he could castigate her, but Sandy thrust a paper before him. Walker hadn't seen him turn up. He looked at the student then down at the report and snatched it from his hand and read it.

'Just as I thought. An abnormality in the temporal lobe.'

'What does it mean, boss?' asked Sandy, his bespectacled eyes intent.

'I'll show you what it means.' Walker turned to Jennifer who had watched the interaction. 'Jenny, can you get a ten-mill syringe.' Walker flicked a hand at Gloria. 'Where's Mr Young?'

Gloria led the way, with Walker, Sandy and Jenny in tow. The young man looked perfectly normal and stuck his arm out obligingly when Walker asked him.

'We just want some blood to find out what's wrong,' Walker said stiffly. He knew it was rude being abrupt with the patient but he couldn't help himself.

Five minutes later, Walker, Gloria and Sandy were walking towards the pathology laboratories. They crossed the air bridge and Walker followed the signs to immunology, which was tucked away in the far corner of the pathology building. He entered the lab and caught the attention of a young technician who had the appearance of a boy-scout leader.

'Chris,' he called. 'Long time no see. What are you up to?'

'Hi, Dave. Got some blood for you. Do you have any monkey brain?'

Dave looked surprised but then gave a knowing look. 'Another one? Well, let's see, smarty pants. Give me the blood.'

Walker leaned against the bench as Gloria and Sandy watched the technician go about his work with energetic but precise movements. He took out a microscope slide that had a brown blob already on the middle but no coverslip and he washed the patient's blood over it repeatedly. Next, he drew out a measure of a solution with a pipette from a flask that had been stored in a fridge nearby. He washed the slide with the solution, then did the same again with a third solution.

Finally, he carried the slide to a microscope nearby. 'Hit that light will you, young chap?' Dave said to Sandy, who did so, throwing the lab into darkness. Dave leaned over the microscope and adjusted the aperture, then the focus, with fine movements. After a moment, he whistled. 'Two out of two, Chris. Very impressive.'

Walker had a quick look down the microscope. He was both pleased and relieved, realising he hadn't been as confident about the diagnosis as he first thought.

'Have a look,' he said to Gloria. He'd lost some of the anger he had felt before but was still annoyed with her.

As she placed her thick glasses against the dual ocular lens, Gloria asked, 'What am I looking at?'

'See those green blobs?' said Dave. 'They're antibodies that have bound to the monkey brain.'

'So?' she said.

'I washed the monkey brain with the patient's blood. Then I washed the brain with an antibody against human immunoglobulin.'

'An antibody against an antibody?' said Gloria, frowning.

'Precisely,' said Dave. 'And that antibody is conjugated with a fluorescent dye, which are the green blobs you can see down the microscope.'

Gloria stood up, her forehead creased in thought. 'So –'

But Sandy interrupted. 'So, if Mr Young's blood contained any antibodies against brain tissue, they would bind to the monkey brain and then the other fluorescent antibody would bind against *it*, which is what we can see.' He had a triumphant look.

'Anti-neuronal antibodies,' said Walker. 'A paraneoplastic syndrome. The CT was normal but the MRI might be sensitive enough to pick up something if there's been any physical damage from the antibodies.'

'How do they form?' asked Sandy.

'Mr Young's immune system detected the abnormal testicular cancer tissue and identified it as foreign. It's not foreign, of course, but new proteins are unmasked and so Mr Young's antibodies try to eradicate them. But they are similar to proteins in his brain and instead of killing the cancer, which has been removed, they attack the brain tissue.'

'Whoa,' said Sandy. 'That doesn't sound good. Are you sure the cancer is still not there?'

'Probably not,' said Walker. 'But we will check again.'

'Can anything be done about it?' asked Gloria.

'That I'm not sure about.' Walker looked worried. His ire was now gone as he thought of his patient's prognosis. 'I've seen this before. The anti-neuronal antibodies can persist even when the cancer is gone and they keep attacking the brain. We can try plasmapheresis – basically washing the antibodies out of the blood – but I'm not sure it will work.'

The stood silently in a circle for a few moments contemplating the patient's uncertain future before Walker broke their thoughts. 'Well, let's go back and tell Mr Young the *good* news.'

## CHAPTER TWENTY-ONE

THE DAY WAS already hot and sticky at nine in the morning as they gathered at the Northern Districts Crematorium in North Ryde on the day of the funeral.

Angela wore black. Walker thought she might wear another colour – he couldn't remember what Chinese were supposed to do – but she didn't. He wore dark blue, and when all the others turned up in black, he felt self-conscious. He had a black suit in his wardrobe at home and wondered why he hadn't worn it. He had thought about it, but something made him change his mind at the last minute. Maybe he didn't really care what Benjamin Chee thought, even if he was looking down at them at his own funeral.

He stood alone with Angela. There were less than a dozen people present, a few senior hospital administrators and Angela's work colleagues. There were no other relatives and Walker figured Benjamin Chee had no friends, or none who wanted to be seen at his funeral at least.

The small group gathered outside the chapel, clustered together in the shade of a large flame tree making small talk, the red flowers of the tree carpeting the ground as if they'd just missed a wedding. Barry Darling was there, as was Constable Jones, tall and looking strangely pious, his uniform ironed and spotless.

Cassandra arrived in her white Mazda RX7 and they all watched as she twisted her long legs out of the car, stood and pulled her tight black dress down before coming to join

Darling and Jones. She waved to Walker and Angela but remained talking to the policemen, which he was glad for. He hadn't spoken to her since the other night in the pub and when he finally did, he didn't want Angela to be there.

Angela and Walker had not spoken about the night they had spent together. He still couldn't reconcile the passion and sexual energy she'd shown, with the demure Asian girl who now stood beside him. He couldn't shake the feeling that there was something wrong about it all. He wanted to talk to her about her feelings, but her father's funeral was definitely the wrong time.

Just before they were ushered into the chapel, Walker was surprised to see Sandy Fuk turn up on a motorbike. He left his helmet and leather jacket near the front door of the chapel and came to sit in the row just behind Angela while Walker sat by her side. He thought it strange that her friend Cassandra remained distant and wondered what they'd spoken about since Angela had been released on bail. An image of Cassandra's long legs flashed into his mind and he batted it away.

The ceremony was short, with just a few prayers from a priest before the coffin was taken away for cremation. There was no eulogy. Apparently, no one wanted to give one.

Afterwards, most people left quickly but Angela lingered with Walker and a few others. Cassandra asked whether there was going to be a wake. Angela said no but would be pleased if they wanted to join her for a cup of tea at her father's place in Epping. Darling said that would be a good idea; he had some news to share and he wanted them together. Sandy gave his apologies, saying he had work to do, but Walker and Cassandra agreed to come back with Angela.

An hour later, they were gathered together in the lounge room of Benjamin Chee's house – Cassandra and Darling sitting together on the lounge, Angela and Walker on the armchairs, and Jones perched stiffly on a kitchen chair he'd dragged into the room. Angela had made a pot of tea, which sat on a marble coffee table in the middle along with a packet of Tim Tams, already melting in the heat. When the tea was distributed, they all looked at Darling expectantly, although annoyingly he said nothing and chatted to Cassandra about the old-style plasterwork of the ceiling.

Finally, Walker interrupted. 'Okay, Wendy, what's this all about? Have you worked out who did it? Is this some sort of Agatha Christie thing?'

At first Darling gave a look of feigned surprise, but then seeing the looks he was getting, he stood up and took a place in the centre of the room, cleared his throat and pulled out his notepad from his pocket, looking for all the world like a television detective about to crack the case. Walker gave a short laugh, which drew a stern look from Darling.

'This relates to evidence that we found in this very room, which I feel has a significant impact on Chee's death.'

He looked at Angela and then back at his notes. He cleared his throat again. Walker thought the whole procedure was a bit contrived.

'It relates to the photos that were housed in that cabinet there.' He pointed to the curved glass cabinet that contained the Lladro figures. 'In particular, the black-and-white photo of Benjamin Chee when he was younger, with two other gentlemen.'

Darling looked from face to face of those in the room.

'Why are you being so melodramatic, Wendy?' asked Walker.

The detective ignored him. 'We faxed the photo to Singapore police. Their Criminal Intelligence found the photo very interesting. Very interesting indeed. And they have been a veritable wealth of information.'

Darling smiled widely at Walker as if he had just countered his comment. He seemed supremely pleased with himself.

'They have identified all three men.' He held up the photo and pointed to the man on the right. 'This is Professor Chee in his younger days, of course.' Then he pointed to the man on the far left. 'Now this man is very interesting. His name was –' he looked down at his notes, 'Chin Peng, the leader of the Malayan National Liberation Army – the MNLA, the military arm of the Malayan Communist Party. And the man in the middle was called Siu Mah, who was also a minor leader of the MNLA.' Darling looked up from his notes at Angela. 'Dr Chee, did you know your father was a member of the Malayan Communist Party?'

She shook her head with a curious expression. 'I had no idea.'

Darling put down the photo and examined his notes as if preparing to give a lecture. 'Apparently, the MNLA triggered the Malayan Emergency after World War Two. Does anyone know what that was?' Seeing blank faces all around, he continued like a schoolteacher before a group of bored students. 'The MNLA fought with the British against the Japanese during the war. But when the Japs were beaten, they expected the Brits to leave. But they didn't, so the communists started a civil war. But they couldn't call it a war for insurance purposes, do you believe it? They called it an "emergency". But a war it certainly was, between the Malayan communists and the British, and the Malayans who supported them. And Chin Peng here was their leader.' Darling picked up the photo and pointed again to the man on the left of the photo, a fellow of obvious Chinese extraction with prominent ears.

'Which leads me to the other fellow, Siu Mah.' Darling pointed to the man in the middle, a gaunt Chinese gentleman, younger than the first. 'Siu Mah was one of the unit leaders in the war. He led the group that ambushed the then British high commissioner, killing him in 1951. The Brits went ballistic about it, trying to find him, but never did. But in 1959, Siu Mah was killed by his own bodyguards and his body handed over to the British after they put a bounty on his head.'

He paused and looked at each face meaningfully. 'And the guy who shot Siu Mah was a fellow called Tek Pou. He subsequently went to Singapore. There, he was married in 1961 and had a child. But in 1975 Pou was forced to leave Singapore on suspicion of being a Communist Party supporter.' He smiled. 'And you know where Tek Pou went to?'

Walker grimaced and shrugged his shoulders. 'Australia?'

Darling pointed a finger at Walker's chest. 'You are correct, Kit. Top marks for listening.'

Cassandra sighed. 'This is all very interesting, Barry. But I assume you're going to tell us the relevance of this history lesson?'

'Oh, it's interesting all right. Because Tek Pou, the man who murdered Siu Mah – the man he was supposed to be guarding – changed his name before he came to Australia.' He looked around expectantly.

Walker pointed at the photo that Darling now held up before his chest. 'Are you telling us that Tek Pou was the third man in the photo?'

'I am indeed.'

Angela stared at the photo, her eyes wide. 'My father?'

'Tek Pou and Benjamin Chee are one and the same man,' announced Darling with great satisfaction.

There was a pause as the audience pondered the implications. Cassandra was the first to speak.

'But what has this all to do with Professor Chee's murder? Are you telling us that it was revenge? Siu Mah's relatives or the communists? But that's preposterous.'

'We haven't ruled out any of those,' Darling said quickly.

Walker noticed the way Darling had responded and smiled to himself. You didn't think of either of those possibilities at all, did you, Wendy? His smile broadened when Darling quickly scribbled a line at the bottom of his notes.

Darling looked up at Angela. 'What I want to know was how much of this was known to Angela Chee about her father.'

'I knew nothing of it. Except that he came from Malaysia and married my mother in Singapore and then had me. And that we came to Australia in 1975. I knew nothing about his involvement with the MNLA or the communists.'

'Nothing? You never wondered? Or guessed?'

'Why would I? He certainly never told me. Nor did my mother.'

'Are you sure you didn't find out recently? It would have made you even angrier with him.'

'Angrier? Angrier than knowing that he caused my mother's death?'

'You knew she died from AIDS?'

She shook her head, her face twisted with old memories. 'Not at the time. But I'm a specialist physician, Detective Darling. It didn't take much to patch the story together. A perfectly healthy woman dying from an overwhelming pneumonia in the mid 1980s? If I couldn't work that out, I don't deserve to be a specialist.'

'So that made you angry with your father?'

'What do you think?' she snapped sarcastically.

'It would have made *me* very angry,' said Darling.

Strangely, Walker thought he looked exactly that – angry. As he spoke, he seemed to become more agitated.

'Your father forced your mother to have sex with other men and one of them gave her AIDS and she died from it.' He glared at the young doctor, his face suffused with anger. 'If my father did that to my mother, I can tell you now – I would have killed him.'

Walker intervened. 'Steady on, Wendy. Angela doesn't need to be dragged into your childhood.'

Darling spun towards Walker. 'What would you know of it, Kit? You had a father and your own home. You don't know the beginning of it.' He clenched his fists and looked down at the carpet, his chest heaving, and slowly, he visibly calmed himself. 'As I was saying, I think it would be natural for anyone who saw their mother go through such a thing to be very angry about it.'

'Angry doesn't begin to describe it, Detective Darling.' Angela's voice was now soft, Darling's outburst having seemed to have calmed her. 'I hated my father for it. I wanted him dead. I'm glad he's dead and I hope he rots for an eternity in hell. I hope there is a God and I pray that He is not a forgiving one. I pray that He punishes my father for what he has done, for ever and ever.'

'Amen,' said Cassandra.

Angela looked at Walker, then Cassandra, and finally back to Darling. 'But I didn't kill him.' She looked away. 'Maybe I should have.'

'So where does this all leave us then?' asked Cassandra.

Walker met Cassandra at the Epping pub and they sat beside each other at one of the tables scattered around the bar, their legs and arms touching. Walker wondered fleetingly about the familiarity. Maybe there was something about a funeral that encouraged personal intimacy. He took a sip of his beer while he thought about it. Or maybe he just liked her.

The gathering at Professor Chee's house had just ended and those present had parted ways. Angela had said she was exhausted and wanted to go home, and gave her apologies when Cassandra suggested they go to the pub. Darling had hesitated but after one look at Walker and then at Jones, who looked on primly listening to their conversation, the detective had said he needed to get back to the station.

Cassandra had a schooner of beer before her, saying she preferred it over wine during the day. 'Otherwise, I get drunk too quickly and become useless for anything else,' she said.

Walker wanted to ask *What else?* but stopped himself, and for a while they sat in companionable silence.

'Who do you think the murderer is?' Cassandra finally asked. She didn't seem particularly interested in the answer. She could have been asking who he thought might win the football on Saturday.

'Who do *you* think?' Walker asked in the same indolent way.

Cassandra became more alert, sitting up in her chair, wiggling her shapely hips as she got more comfortable. 'Let's see if we can work it out. We've got all the information. We're clever. I'm a lawyer and you're a doctor. Between us, we have a better chance than Barry. To be honest, although he's cute, he's not the sharpest tool in the shed.'

Walker let out a laugh. 'I'll agree with you there.' Then he became more reflective. 'Maybe we can. Let's put our heads together.'

Cassandra got an eager look and shuffled closer and actually put her long blonde locks against his head. Walker could feel her ear against his and her breast pushed into his shoulder. Her hand slipped along his thigh. 'Okay.' She sounded excited.

Walker tried to focus but it took some moments before he could collect his thoughts. He struggled to shut out the pleasure of her hand caressing his leg above the knee.

Finally he spoke, trying to sound like a TV detective. 'We have three murders: Professor Chee, Sanjeev the pharmacist, and Andy the wardsman. Let's take them one at a time – Professor Chee first.'

He could feel Cassandra nod her head.

'We have to admit,' he continued in a sensible tone, 'that Angela could have murdered her father. He was a total sleazebag and what he did to Angela's mother was enough excuse, if you were looking for one. She had a bag of metoprolol, the drug that was found in Chee's blood, in large amounts, enough to kill him.'

'But Chee also had pancuronium in his blood and there was no evidence of Angela having any of that.'

Walker was glad Cassandra was taking the matter seriously. For a moment, he'd thought he would have to do all the talking. 'She could have used it all up and had nothing to discard. Remember, I found the ampoule on Chee's bed.'

She pulled away and turned her face to him but kept her hand on his leg. 'Whose side are you on?'

'We have to put our feelings for Angela aside if we're going to get to the bottom of it.'

'This is harder than it looks. I'm not sure we *can* get to the bottom of it, after all.'

'Okay, okay. But let's keep going. We might work out something helpful.'

She put her head against his again. Walker smiled to himself at the action. It was so deliciously childish.

'Let's see then,' he said, frowning. 'Andy had pancuronium in his blood, just like Chee.'

'Angela couldn't have killed Andy since she was in jail.'

'Granted.'

They sat quietly for a few moments. Walker tried to think but now Cassandra's head and body were subtly wriggling in time with the music that came from a pub speaker overhead. With a grimace, Walker recognised the song – Chrissy Amphlett touching herself again in that sultry voice of hers. The same song that had triggered the carnal reaction in Angela the other night.

Amphlett's trying to ruin me! He struggled to focus on the conversation. 'What about Sanjeev? Whoever killed him could drive a forklift. Can Angela drive one?'

Cassandra shrugged. 'Don't know. I doubt it.'

'Whoever killed Sanjeev probably did it because Sanjeev found out about the pancuronium missing from the endoscopy suite. Maybe he worked out who it was?'

'I reckon a wardsman could drive a forklift. Maybe Andy killed Sanjeev?'

'So that would mean Andy killed Chee. Why? There was that business with the Freemasons but that's hardly reason to kill Chee. If anything, it would be the other way around – Chee killing Andy because the Masons found out about Chee's perversions. Andy could have got the drugs. But how would he know which drugs to use? And how is a wardsman going to cannulate?'

Cassandra pulled the corners of her lips down. 'And who killed *him*?'

Walker took a swig of his beer, finishing it. 'This is getting us nowhere.' He raised his empty glass. 'Want another?'

'My shout,' said Cassandra. 'Same again?'

Walker watched her walk towards the bar and noticed how many heads turned to follow her progress – male and female. Her short tight black dress could have been for a cocktail party rather than a funeral.

She noticed him studying her as she returned from the bar, holding two schooners of beer. Her eyes locked onto his and she smiled. He smiled back. He should have felt guilty. She was going out with his ex-best friend and Walker had only just slept with Angela. But he didn't care. Maybe it was the beer. Maybe it was the funeral. Whatever the reason, he felt good being with her. He was having fun.

She sat down beside him and cuddled close, her hand slipping to his leg again. 'Where were we, Sherlock?'

He laughed and placed his hand on her bare leg just below her hem. 'Let's see, Watson. I think we've almost cracked it.'

'What's our next move then?'

Walker hesitated. He was enjoying the flirting but he wasn't sure he wanted to go any further. 'Well, I think we should go back to basics,' he said slowly. He took his hand off her thigh and lifted his glass to his lips. 'Chee had a lot of enemies. McBrent could have been worried Chee would tell his wife. Perhaps Chee was blackmailing him?'

'Do you think that's possible?'

'McBrent is a total wanker and he's got a terrible temper.' He paused in thought. 'But I don't see him poisoning anyone. I doubt he could even get a cannula in. Besides, poisoning is too subtle for him. Beating someone to death with a phonebook is more his style.'

Cassandra giggled. 'What about this Malayan communist thing? It's hard to believe that Chee was ever a bodyguard. But maybe it's simply revenge for killing one of their leaders.'

Walker murmured his agreement. 'We have to keep coming back to the fact that whoever the killer is, they have to know about drugs and how to put a cannula in. That narrows it down.'

'What about that skinny Malaysian dude. What's his name? Sandy. He could be a communist?'

Walker smirked. 'A communist assassin who became a medical student and tracked Chee down, then got a position in the hospital so he could kill him? Sounds a bit far-fetched.'

'Well, maybe he's not a medical student at all. Maybe he's just a communist assassin?'

Walker shook his head. 'He knows too much medicine. His knowledge is quite impressive for a student, actually.'

'It just sounds too much of a coincidence that Chee had a dark past in Malaysia and was murdered right when a Malaysian student turns up in the hospital.'

'You might have something there.' He was getting tired of thinking about it. It was clear they weren't going to crack the case.

Cassandra took a long sip of her beer then turned her face so her mouth was close to his ear. She dropped her voice. 'Maybe it was you. Maybe you killed Chee, then you knocked off the pharmacist, then Andy, to cover your tracks.'

Walker pulled away and examined her face to see whether she was serious. But instead, all he could think of was how attractive she looked. Her red lips were curled into a mischievous smile. She licked her top lip.

'Why would I kill Chee?'

She raised her eyebrows. 'For Angela?'

'Why for Angela? I hardly know her.'

'Do you? But you want her, I can tell by the way you look at her.' She leaned back and pulled her hair off her shoulders, a movement that exaggerated her breasts in the tight black funeral dress. 'Angela's told me about you. Your wife. She died six years ago. I bet you've not had a woman since.' Walker looked away. She leaned forward again. 'Angela's attractive. You could have wanted it so much that you'd do anything for it. Even kill her father.'

'That's ridiculous,' he said, his voice low.

'Is it? Some people would do anything for sex. I would. When I get horny, nothing stands in my way.'

Walker glanced around the pub. No one was looking at them. 'Are you horny now?'

Walker felt her lips touch his ear then the sharp pain of her teeth nipping his earlobe.

'Sherlock, tell me something,' she breathed. 'What is it about funerals? They always make me want to have a man between my legs. Something about realising my own mortality.' He felt her wet tongue in his ear. 'Don't worry about Angela. She's too complicated. If all you want is sex, pure and simple – uncomplicated – then have me.'

She pulled away and moved so her face was close to his. He could feel her breath on his mouth. 'We've had a hard few weeks. I really think we should console each other.'

Her soft lips touched his. He offered no resistance. Her tongue gently parted his lips.

'Where can we go?' he asked. 'Angela will be at your flat.'

'Your place.'

'It'll take forty minutes to get there.'

Her hand moved up his thigh. 'Don't worry, I'll keep you in the mood.'

## CHAPTER TWENTY-TWO

WALKER STOOD AT the nurses' station and punched numbers into the phone, an irritated look on his face. Angela was still not allowed to return to work, so he would have to do the ward round with his intern and he wasn't in the mood for her bumbling incompetence. He threw the handset down on the cradle, drawing looks from the nurses.

'Get out the wrong side of the bed today, did you, Chris?' asked Jenny, lightly touching his shoulder.

'What do you mean?'

He had spent the night with Cassandra and could still sense her skin against his, her moisture, her energy. For some reason, he'd always thought that very attractive women would be sexually lazy, expecting everything and giving nothing. But Cassandra Hollow was a real firecracker. He hadn't told Cassandra that he'd slept with Angela, and they had parted that morning with a promise to keep their liaison secret. Guiltily, he mentally compared them. They were so different in appearance but both so sexually spirited. Were all women like that? Flea hadn't been. They had enjoyed each other's bodies but he couldn't remember them ever experiencing the frenetic heat he'd had with both Angela and Cassandra.

Jenny was studying his face closely. 'You look different,' she said. Now she had a cheeky smile. 'What have you been up to?'

How did she know?

'Nothing,' he spluttered. 'Have you seen Gloria? I have to do the bloody round with her.'

Jenny's eyes flashed over his shoulder and he turned to see his intern walking towards them, looking down as she read her pager. The way her thick orange hair sat on the top of her hair like a mop-head made him even more irritated and he let out a noisy, exasperated breath.

Gloria looked up. 'Oh, Dr Walker! Did you page me?'

'Can we do a round?' he asked flatly.

'Of course. Where do you want to start?'

'You're in charge,' said Walker, his voice devoid of confidence. 'Lead the way.'

As they moved towards the first patient, Gloria stopped, and her bearing became mournful.

'I can't get over the news about Andy,' she gushed. 'Why would anyone do that?'

'Yes, terrible,' muttered Walker.

'How did he die?'

Her doleful eyes raised his ire and he snapped. 'Pancuronium. He was pumped full of pancuronium.' Walker wondered whether she'd even know what it was.

'But that's terrible,' she gasped. 'What an awful way to die. Just lying there completely alert and not able to move or breathe. Horrible!'

Walker merely grunted and motioned her to get on with it. But she stood her ground. 'He was such a nice fellow. He'd go out of his way to help anyone. Even agreed to let Sandy practice his cannulation skills on him.'

Walker moved around her towards the first bed bay then he stopped abruptly. 'Cannulation skills?' He spun around. 'When was that?'

'Four days ago. Andy was on the evening shift and agreed to let Sandy have a go if it got quiet enough. I saw them having dinner together.'

'In the cafeteria?'

'Of course, where else is there?'

Walker thought quickly. The cafeteria was directly below the lecture theatres where Korbmann's body was found.

'Where's Sandy now?'

'Gone about ten minutes ago. Said he was meeting Angela at her place.' Gloria threw up her hands. 'Even she's in on it now. No one helped me so much when I was a medical student. She said he could practise on her.'

'Practise? His cannulation?'

Walker took the stairs two at a time until he reached the bottom floor and sprinted along the corridor at breakneck speed, reached the electric doors and slammed into the glass. They'd failed to open again! He jumped back and waved his hands above his head and set off again when they finally opened, racing across the courtyard to the next building. He finally reached the external entrance of the hospital near the car park where there was an alcove where motorbikes were often parked. He flung the door outwards and it slammed against the brick wall. Facing away from him was Sandy, revving the engine of his bike.

'Sandy! Stop!' screamed Walker.

But either Sandy couldn't hear him over the roar of the engine with his helmet on or he ignored him, Walker couldn't be sure. But he raced off up the road, a puff of smoke spurting from the exhaust, and was soon out of view.

Walker sprinted back through the entrance and along the corridor to the oncology clinics and picked up the first phone. Two nurses who had been tidying up the clinic watched him wide-eyed as he stabbed the buttons on the phone while he struggled to balance a notebook on his arm, reading a number as he dialled.

'I need to speak to Detective Darling right away,' he yelled when it was finally answered. 'Yes, it's urgent. It's about the recent murders.'

Walker knocked his knuckles on the desktop impatiently while he waited.

'Wendy, I know who it is.'

'Who?'

'Sandy.'

Darling sounded puzzled. 'Who?'

'The Malaysian student. Just believe me. I'll tell you the full story but right now he's going to Angela's place and I think he's going to poison her, like the others.'

'I'll meet you there in ten.'

Walker flung the phone receiver back onto its cradle and sprinted back towards the car park with the two astonished nurses staring after him.

Walker burned along Pennant Hills Road, weaving in and out of the evening traffic on his way to Epping. Up ahead the lights were red and the two lanes were full of waiting cars as he pulled up. At the head of the traffic, waiting at the lights, was a motorbike. Walker recognised the helmet.

Sandy!

For a moment he considered pulling out onto the wrong side of the road but just as he decided to do it, the lights turned green and oncoming traffic barrelled towards him. He heard the chain-saw buzz of Sandy's Honda tear away from the lights. Walker swore and impatiently gunned his engine as each car took off one at a time, seemingly in slow motion.

'Come on!' he shouted.

Finally, the traffic on the opposite side cleared so he put his foot down and jerked onto the wrong side of the road, feeling the satisfying push of leather into his back as the six cylinders roared. Fifty metres away, a semitrailer was coming towards him. With the tachometer pushed as far as it would go and still in third, he swerved back into the lane just before the semi reached him, air horn blaring.

Sirens wailing, Darling sped along Kissing Point Road in the left-hand lane towards Epping, the speedometer reading one hundred and fifty kilometres per hour. Suddenly, a startled driver swerved in front of him trying to get out of the way and he jammed on the brakes. He jabbed his right foot down and the car lurched forward again, the engine roaring.

'Yeeee!' howled Cassandra, finishing her exclamation with an elated whoop. 'Wow, this car is fantastic!' She had one fist tight around her seatbelt and the other hand on the dashboard, her eyes wide with excitement. 'Can you go faster?'

Darling took a left onto Marsden, the siren still throbbing, and veered onto the right-hand side of the road to go around the traffic stopped at the lights, then took a right onto Terry. The road was clear and he let the beast have its head, hitting one-seventy as he neared Midson, where he took a left. The car sped through the backstreets of Epping but as he approached Angela's flat, he killed the siren and coasted to a stop outside a four-storey blond-brick apartment block. In the driveway was a Honda trail bike. Sandy was nowhere to be seen. As they got out of the car, Walker pulled up behind.

They reached the front door of Angela's flat with Walker just in front.

'There's no handle,' hissed Walker. 'We'll have to break it down. Come on, Wendy.' He stepped backwards and pulled Darling to his side. 'On the count of three ...'

'Stop, you idiots,' said Cassandra. 'I live here, remember. Step aside.'

She plunged the key into the lock and turned it and Walker pushed past, bursting the door open. 'Angela!'

Cassandra ran ahead along the hall and stopped in a doorway. Her hand went to her mouth and Walker and Darling looked over her shoulder.

On the bed, unmoving and unbreathing, was Angela. Dead. There was a cannula in her left forearm.

'We're too late,' Cassandra cried.

'Move,' Walker shouted as he squeezed past. He kneeled beside the bed and felt for a pulse in her neck. Darling and Cassandra watched wordlessly. 'She's alive,' he hissed. 'Paralysed. Pancuronium for sure. She can probably hear us.' He leaned over her and placed his mouth against hers and puffed, then he looked at her face. Then he started breathing into her mouth again.

'Sandy's killed her, the bastard,' Cassandra screamed.

'He's got to be here somewhere,' said Darling.

'Call the ambulance,' Walker yelled over his shoulder between breaths.

The front door slammed.

'Sandy!' Darling cried in alarm. 'It's gotta be him. I'm going after him.'

He ran from the room. Cassandra looked towards Angela and then in the direction Darling had taken. She moved away.

'I'll call from the car,' she called as she ran.

Walker covered Angela's mouth with his, pulling her jaw down to open her airway, and breathed out as fast as he could. He wanted to talk to her, comfort her, but he knew he didn't have the time. If she'd only been injected with pancuronium she would be paralysed but fully alert. Her heart was still beating, he could feel it against his chest, rustling like a small animal. He breathed out and sucked in another breath. He was beginning to feel dizzy. Would she be panicking? Of course, she would!

'Don't worry, Angela, I'll keep you alive until help arrives,' he gasped.

It would have to be enough. He pushed more air into her lungs. If only he had the right equipment. How many people had he resuscitated in his time? Over a hundred? Most had not survived, but they hadn't been young fit women. If only he had a bag and mask. And some oxygen.

Shut up and keep breathing.

Breathe in deeply. Push the air into her lungs. She was paralysed; there was no resistance so it was easy. Is she still alive? He stopped and felt for a pulse in her neck. Nothing.

He ripped her top away and placed his ear on her left breast. Pump, pump. She was alive!

He started again. Breathe. Breathe. Sorry for stopping, Angela. Trust your clinical instincts. I can do this. I can save her. I'll keep going until they get here. If Cassandra has called them!

He put his lips against hers. He'd wanted to do this again but not like this. Keep going. Don't stop for anything. Her lips were cold. Keep going. She will live. She didn't do it. She didn't kill her father. It was Sandy. She's innocent. And me? What about me?

He stopped abruptly.

Keep going. Breathe. Breathe.

Flea's gone. Angela must live.

He almost stopped again. He forced himself to keep going. Had Flea wanted to die? Did Angela? Breathe. Breathe.

There was a hand on his shoulder. Was Wendy back? Was it Flea? Did she want him to stop? But he wouldn't. He brushed her hand away.

'Move aside,' said a male voice. Hands grabbed him and pulled him away. He struggled but then he saw them. Paramedics. They had a mask and a bag and oxygen.

Walker pushed back against the wall and covered his head with his arms.


Darling flipped the switch and the siren wailed. Tyres screeched. Towards the end of the street, a Honda trail bike screamed like a banshee.

'Get the little bastard, Barry,' yelled Cassandra. 'Don't let him get away.'

Darling slapped his foot to the floor. Damned if he'd let him.

But either Sandy knew the roads well or he was lucky since he went straight down Midson Road towards the river and Darling knew what that meant. Speed bumps. Nothing for a trail bike but murder for a high-performance vehicle like his. He doubted the bike could do much more than 120 kph. On the straight, he'd be dead meat. But the speed bumps meant that Darling had to slow down and let the little bugger get away.

He flipped the switch on his radio. 'Suspect heading south on Midson towards Victoria Road. Honda trail bike, black helmet. In pursuit.' He just hoped there would be a patrol car on the road nearby. The Ryde police station was close. Maybe they were already near.

The bike turned left onto Victoria Road and, with the speed bumps left behind, Darling thought he had him. But there was a break in the traffic and Sandy took the first right.

'Where does that go to?' asked Cassandra.

'Parramatta River.'

Darling accelerated and soon was right on the tail of the Honda. They came to a roundabout and the bike went straight through the middle, taking off into the air from the small rise. Darling had to slow to curve around it.

'It's a no through road,' called Cassandra and Darling jammed on the brakes. 'What are you doing?'

'That goes to Meadowbank Park. We'll lose him. He'll drive straight over the fields,' Darling yelled over the roar of the V8 as he did a quick three-point turn in the narrow street.

'I know it,' said Cassandra. 'I used to play netball there.'

He grunted, then retraced his route, taking the first right along a road that skirted the park.

'He'll have to come out somewhere. The park is hemmed in by the river.'

Darling drove east at a moderate pace, peering into the park between houses at every opportunity.

'I think I saw him,' said Cassandra. 'Down near the river. How far along can he go?'

'I'm pretty sure he'll take the cycleway that runs along the river.'

'Do you think we can catch him?'

'Never fear,' he shouted. '"The Phantom moves faster than a great cat, with the power of a charging bull elephant."'

Cassandra shrieked with delight as Darling opened the throttle and the Commodore lurched forward, rubber burning. They sped through the backstreets of the industrial area of Meadowbank, a row of low factories on the river side of the road and Californian bungalows on the left. The lights were red at Ryde Road, a major transport route that cut the area from north to south. Darling edged his car through the traffic, sirens wailing and lights flashing.

He radioed in. 'Travelling east along Morrison. Suspect is probably on the riverside cycleway east of Ryde Road.' There were a few replies of affirmation but no sightings.

'He'll have to come out soon,' said Darling. 'The cycleway ends at Kissing Point Park.' He sped towards the point and turned into Pelliser, which curved down towards the river.

'Where does this go?'

'The punt.'

There was a flash of red and the Honda jumped out from the bushland on the right-hand side and landed just in front of Darling's car, causing him to slam on the brakes. Sandy almost went over, bouncing into the opposite gutter before coming to a dead stop.

His helmet turned towards them. Darling saw fear in his eyes.

'Sandy,' yelled Darling. 'Give it up. You can't get away.'

Sandy hesitated, then his appearance changed. Darling recognised determination.

The Honda tore off down the slope towards the water.

'After him!' shouted Cassandra and Darling pursued in a squeal of rubber and black smoke.

They rounded the bend but the trail bike was already towards the bottom of the hill. The ferry was just pushing off, a flat boat holding two lanes of three cars with a fixed ramp at both ends, pulled across the channel by a set of cables on each side. The boom gate was down and the ferry was already about twenty metres from shore.

Darling pulled up. Sandy had nowhere to go.

But he gunned the engine and it screamed. Sandy veered to the side of the road where a pile of soil sat after recent roadworks and he hit it at top speed. He took to the air, the bike trajectory forming a perfect arc high above the water, the rider perfectly balanced.

'Bloody hell!' said Darling.

'He's done that before,' Cassandra gasped appreciatively at the same time.

When he told the story later, Darling considered that maybe he would have made it if he was a few seconds earlier. A Honda CR250 trail bike has a maximum jump length of perhaps thirty-five metres under the best conditions. And by the time Sandy took off, the ferry would have been at about that length from the shore. But the conditions were far from perfect, and so subsequently, he fell short by a few metres.

The bike opened the waters like Moses parting the Red Sea, creating a fan-shaped splash on both sides. Sandy was thrust over the handlebars and rolled twice over the surface in front of the bike then sank to the bottom.

And didn't come up.

'Do you think he can swim?' said Cassandra.

They waited a few more moments.

'Apparently not,' said Darling. He threw open the door, ran down the ramp, pulled off his jacket and shoes at the water's edge, and dived in. He trod water above the spot where he figured Sandy had sunk, then duck-dived down.

Cassandra watched, holding her breath in sympathy.

Just when she thought she could no longer hold on, Darling's head broke the water's surface. Then he reached down and with a mighty effort, hauled a body up beside him. He swam with one arm towards shore and when he could stand, dragged the body the rest of the way, with Cassandra helping for the last few steps.

They threw him onto the concrete ramp and his body flopped like a dead fish.

Cassandra started mouth-to-mouth.

## CHAPTER TWENTY-THREE

FUK YEH-HAH was propped up in a hospital bed with Darling and Jones on one side and Walker on the other. Outside of the door sat two uniformed police officers. The young man had his head back and eyes closed and could have been asleep.

'Tell us your story, Sandy,' Darling said softly.

For some time, there was silence and Darling glanced at Walker and then Jones, wondering whether he should wake him.

But then Sandy spoke, his eyes still closed. 'Professor Chee was a murderer. He killed my grandfather. He was an evil man. He deserved to die.'

Darling spoke. 'We now know Chee was born Tek Pou in Malaysia. We also know he was the one who shot Siu Mah, the Communist Party leader. But tell us of his connection with your grandfather.'

'My grandfather's name was Fuk Tien Ho. My family are all Straits-born Chinese – Baba. I am Peranakan. We have a proud heritage. My ancestors were among the first to settle in Penang and Malacca from southern China many years ago. Tek Pou's family – Chee's family – were *sinkhek*, newcomers. They came after my ancestors had done all the pioneering work to make the Straits what it is today – or what it was before the war. They are like sponges soaking up the benefits of my ancestors' hard labour.

## Murder on the Ward      199

'My family were the elite. We went to British schools and spoke English and could work closely with the British to allow Malaya to flourish. But the war changed everything. The Japanese invaded us and we lost our homes. Our Nyonyas – our women – had to sell their jewellery and the Babas had to get lowly work to survive.'

He paused as he gave a moist cough. There was a wheeze in his chest when he took a deep breath.

'After the war, my grandfather became the driver for the British High Commissioner. It was a privileged position. My grandfather spoke perfect English and, I'm told, loved his position and was very loyal to his employer.

'But then one day, the dirty communists, led by Siu Mah, ambushed the British High Commissioner in the mountains above Kuala Lumpur. My grandfather was the driver of his Rolls Royce. A Silver Wraith. The commissioner was killed. His wife survived. My grandfather disappeared. At first, the commissioner's private secretary, who had survived the attack, had said that my grandfather was abducted by the communists. But later he changed his story. He said he might have fled *with* the communists. Such a lie!'

Sandy broke into a hacking cough. Unable to speak, he sat forward, his chest rattling between each forced exhalation. Darling looked at Walker nervously. The student was struggling, unable to take a proper breath, and his lips started to turn blue. Walker stepped forward and slapped him on the back and Sandy finally coughed up a plug of green sputum into his hand. Walker offered him a tissue and the student collapsed back onto the bed, exhausted.

Minutes later, when he had recovered, he began again. 'Our family suffered. We were shunned by our own community. My grandmother died of shame. My father was not allowed to go to school and had to move to KL to find work. He is still there now working in a factory. Can you believe it? A Baba from one of the founding families having to scratch out a living in a filthy factory in KL!

'But later we found out the truth. My grandfather had been taken to a jungle camp and was held in a cage. And there he starved. It was the time of the Malayan Emergency and the British were trying to flush out the communists by starving the population. It worked as a strategy. But it also killed my grandfather. Or rather, the animals that locked him up killed him. And that animal was Tek Pou – Professor Chee.'

'How did you find out he was in Australia?' asked Darling.

'I didn't,' said Sandy. 'It was a pure coincidence. I knew that Tek Pou had changed his name. I also knew he had fled to Singapore. But the family did not know he had come to Australia.

'I came to work at the Meadows as part of my medical training. And then one day towards the end of last year, Professor Chee invited me home for tea. I thought he was very kind and welcoming – and he was. He just wanted to talk about Malaysia. I think he missed it. But then I saw the photo. The one sitting on the cabinet in the lounge room. Every one of those men's faces are burned into my mind. When I saw the photo, I realised who Chee really was: Tek Pou, the jailer of my grandfather. His murderer. The man who led to the downfall of my family. The man who caused my proud father to slave away in a dirty factory in Malaysia.'

'It was then I realised he had to die.'

'And how did you go about it?' asked Darling.

Sandy lolled his head back as if he might pass out. He lay for some moments with his eyes closed, breathing deeply. Then he stirred abruptly and his eyes flung open.

'Kill him! What do you mean? Is that what you think? You think I killed him?' He struggled to sit upright.

'What are you talking about?' cried Darling.

'I didn't kill him! Wanted to. But I didn't get to do it. I thought you knew that. I thought you must have found the killer.'

Sandy looked from face to face, his eyes wide, his mouth open like a mullet. 'He was already dead when I found him.'

## Murder on the Ward

'What do you mean?' Darling demanded. 'Are you saying you didn't kill him?'

'Of course I didn't kill him.'

Darling looked dumbly from Sandy to Walker and back again. 'But what about Angela Chee? You tried to kill her.'

'I did not.' His words were emphatic. 'I was practising my cannulation on her. She agreed to it – and I got it in. But when I flushed the cannula, she went all floppy. I thought she had fainted but then I realised she had stopped breathing. I knew I had no chance of resuscitating her by myself so I ran into the lounge room to use the phone to call the ambulance. But then you three burst in and, by the way you were shouting, I could see you were going to blame me.'

'What?' Darling still wore a face of stunned disbelief.

'So I panicked. I made a run for it. I thought you wouldn't even know I was there but the stupid door banged. And when you started chasing me ... well, I just panicked even more.'

'Why did you run?' asked Walker.

'You don't know what it is like in Malaysia. Sometimes the police don't ask questions. They just shoot.'

'Sandy,' said Walker. 'Where did you get the cannula and saline flush to practise on Angela?'

Sandy frowned thinking hard. 'The ward.'

'So you just took a random selection from the tubs?'

'Yes,' said Sandy. 'They're all there in the treatment room. Anyone can take them.'

Walker grimaced at Darling who shook his head.

'Do you expect us to believe –'

'No, wait,' Sandy interrupted, sitting forward. 'I remember now. Someone gave it me. I was about to pick up a pack but another was pushed into my hands.'

'Who gave it to you?' asked Walker, his voice tense.

Sandy spoke a name and a moment later, Darling turned to those present and said in a harsh whisper, 'Tell no one of this.' Then he turned back. 'You say you didn't do it, Sandy. Well, I'm going to give you a chance to prove it.'

Fuk Yeh-Hah was in a deep sleep in the hospital bed, the emotional and physical excitement of the day having finally taken its toll. He breathed easily, although occasionally there was a rattle in his chest, the after-effects of the inhaled river water. The green light of the IMED pump flashed slowly, indicating the drip in his right arm was still patent, infusing his veins with antibiotics to fight off pneumonia from the polluted water of the Parramatta River.

The room was otherwise empty but just outside the door, perched on a chair, was an overweight policeman who was of an age whereby most officers had retired. He sat with arms folded, sleepily watching the nurses go about their work in the dim light of the night-time ward.

The nurses' shift had changed an hour ago and all the patients were settled and asleep so the ward was quiet. A nurse sat at the desk, a steaming cup of tea before her as she flicked through the pages of the latest edition of the *Women's Weekly*. A buzzer sounded and the nurse looked up at the dull green light that showed outside one of the bedbays. With a sigh, she got to her feet, grabbed a flashlight, then made her way to the room. Just after she moved away, a figure slipped past the nurses' station in the gloom and stopped before the policeman.

'Officer,' said a soft voice. 'The nurses asked me to come and get you. They saw a stranger lurking out near the stairwell. They said he looked suspicious.'

The policemen looked apprehensive as he climbed to his feet, as if he wasn't expecting this. He was only posted to make sure the prisoner didn't escape. He stuck his head in the door and saw that Sandy was in a deep sleep then turned back to the person who had addressed him. In the dark of the ward, he couldn't properly see the face. The person wore surgical scrubs and cap and had a paper mask pulled up over the mouth. 'Whereabouts did you say?' He didn't look keen.

## Murder on the Ward

'In the corridor, just before the stairs. Out through the double doors.'

With a grunt, he waddled off up the corridor, unfastening the safety strap on his holster as he went.

The figure entered the dim room. There was soft rustle, then a syringe appeared in a gloved hand. The other hand felt along the IV line until the bung was found. In less than a breath, the bung was punctured and the contents of the syringe were pumped into the saline and into Sandy's vein.

There was a click and the room was flooded with light, causing the figure to spin around in alarm.

'So it *was* you,' said Walker with amazement.

The person blinked in the bright light and pushed a bushy orange fringe back away from her eyes. The mask had fallen to reveal thick lips turned down in what Walker thought was disappointment rather than the fear he had expected. She glanced down at Sandy with a knowing grimace, which changed to suspicion when he sat upright, too spritely for someone who'd just been poisoned.

'What's going on?' she said. Then she reached down and pulled back the bedcovers to display the IV line. The plastic tube ended in a rolled-up towel. 'What sort of a trick is this?' she demanded.

'Are you kidding?' said Darling. 'We just witnessed you attempting to murder this man.'

Gloria let out an irritated breath. 'All right then.' She sounded peeved. 'If this is the way it must be, so be it.'

The policeman returned and now, in the light of the room, was no longer the geriatric he'd appeared to be. Constable Jones moved to Gloria and put his hand on her shoulder. Walker could see he had put grey colouring through his hair and wore padding beneath his uniform.

'You are under arrest for the attempted murder of Fuk Yeh-Hah,' said Jones. 'You are not obliged to say or do anything unless you wish to do so.'

'But why?' interrupted Walker. 'Why did you kill Professor Chee?'

'Why?' she snapped. 'Are you kidding? You know what he did to his wife. The more important question is, why didn't his daughter do it? The gutless bitch.'

'Take her away, Jones,' said Darling. 'We'll finish this back at the station.'

---

Gloria sat slumped in her seat in the second-floor interview room of the Parramatta Area Command, her lawyer beside her, a thin, bemused young man with premature balding; a distant relative, according to the intern.

Constable Jones had already informed her of her rights and the interview was underway.

Gloria's thick lips were turned down as usual, which made her appear more as if she was displeased with her meal in a restaurant rather than fighting a murder charge. Her thick orange hair sat on top of her head and she stared through her glasses at Detective Darling as if he was speaking another language.

But she seemed to understand his question about her method of murder since she answered without hesitation, as if she was pleased to tell her audience of her achievements.

'It is really quite easy to murder someone in a hospital, you know,' she said. She looked from Darling to Jones as if they might disagree with her, then continued. 'I stole a box of pancuronium from the endoscopy suite and metoprolol from CCU. They are not narcotics so are not kept under lock and key.' She raised her hands as if the mere ease with which the drugs could be obtained were reason enough to kill someone. 'And then I waited for the right moment. And that moment came when Chee was admitted for his thyroid treatment.

'I entered his room and said he needed a cannula. It was funny. He didn't even question it – just held out his arm. Then I injected the pancuronium. He was paralysed. It was touch and go. But I've done two terms of anaesthetics as a medical student so I sort of knew what I was doing. I gave him just enough so he couldn't move but could still breathe – just. My old anaesthetics boss would have been proud of me.

'And then I made him listen to what he had done to Lucia. My friend. My very good friend. Sweet Lucia.'

Now she had tears in her eyes.

'Do you know we were neighbours? I lived up the street from her when I worked at Channel Seven and we would often have coffee. We became good friends and I could sense there was something wrong. And then one day she told me the whole story. The whole filthy tale. How her rotten husband made her sleep with other men. And how one of the filthy bastards gave her AIDS. And soon after, she was dead. It killed her in the end ... he killed her. He deserved to die.

'So, I told him Lucia's story from her point of view. Made him listen to it. I couldn't tell whether he was sorry but it is my firm wish and hope that he was very frightened – just like Lucia would have been when she was gasping and sweating in that hospital bed just before she died. When I'd finished my story, I injected two ampoules of metoprolol to stop his heart. Just in case someone came in and resuscitated him. I'm so glad I did that.' She raised her eyebrows. 'Otherwise, Dr Walker might have saved him.'

'But why the pharmacist, Sanjeev, and Andy Korbmann?' asked Darling. 'They didn't do anything.'

Gloria dropped her head. 'That was very sad.' She sounded sincere. 'They were innocent. But Andy saw me in endoscopy. He came in when I was going through the anaesthetic trolley. He might not have realised what I was doing at the time but the more I thought about it, I realised I couldn't take the chance. Eventually, I decided he had to go.'

'And Sanjeev?' asked Darling.

'He'd just done a stocktake of the endoscopy unit. I knew he realised the pancuronium was gone and he would have been able to work out when it happened. And it would be easy to track who'd entered using their pass on those days. I'd gone down to pharmacy to deal with him and overheard him speaking on the phone to Dr Walker. I knew he hadn't disclosed my name but I was sure he was about to. I had to work quickly. Luckily, I'd learned to drive a forklift while working in my other job before I did medicine. You know I was a set designer for Channel Seven?' She looked at Darling then grimaced at his lack of reaction. 'I even told Dr Walker but he didn't care. Nobody cares about an old intern.

'Anyway, at Channel Seven, I often had to do the whole damn thing myself. Couldn't rely on help so I learned to drive a forklift. Not very well, but enough to move things around when I needed to. But that was a long time ago now.'

'But why Angela?' asked Darling. 'She wasn't a risk to you.'

Gloria smiled. 'That was just me being too clever. She's sweet but she wasn't a good daughter to her mother. If that was my mother, and knowing what Angela knew, I would have killed Chee a long time ago. But she didn't have the guts. She knew about it but she did nothing. So I had to do her dirty work. I was beginning to think she was more like her father than her mother. I decided she also had to die.'

'And Sandy?'

'Well, he was just a smart-arse, making me look bad all the time. So, when he told me he was practising on Angela I got the idea to frame him. I gave him the cannulation pack. It was easy to suck all the saline out of the plastic ampoule and replace it with pancuronium. If Angela died, then Sandy would have been blamed and I would have got off scot-free.'

'So you killed three people, tried to murder Angela and aimed to frame Sandy?' said Darling.

Gloria's lips curled into a smile. 'Dr Walker thinks I'm stupid but I'm not so stupid after all, am I?' She raised her eyebrows. 'I bet he couldn't have juggled the dose of pancuronium like I did, to keep Professor Chee paralysed but still breathing.' She laughed. 'He was always so superior with his clever diagnoses, the clubbing and the paraneoplastic syndromes. But I murdered his colleague right under his nose and he couldn't even work it out.'

She stood and thrust her hands towards Jones as if she was already handcuffed. 'Arrest me, constable. Do your worst. I *know* what I did was right and proper and no one will take that away from me.'


Walker was waiting in the corridor just outside the interview room and Gloria, now in handcuffs and led by Jones, stopped before him. Her face twisted into a sneer.

'You think you do so much for your patients but you do nothing for them. Most of them die. You just torture them for a bit beforehand. And then you let them die. How is that so different to what I did?' She threw back her head contemptuously. 'The big difference is that those poor souls have done nothing wrong. They don't deserve to die but they do. You can't stop it. Chee was a monster. More than a monster. Why in heaven's name should *he* be allowed to live while in the same ward, those poor innocent and good people die like animals?'

Walker watched as she was led away and thought of what she'd said. Deep down he knew she was right. He really didn't help his patients that much. Worse, he'd done something that was more despicable than what she had done. He couldn't say a word as she left.

He had let his wife die.

All he could feel was the Black beginning to form a chasm within his chest.

## CHAPTER TWENTY-FOUR

WALKER TURNED UP to work three days later, having taken a few sickies, something he rarely did. He'd spent the first two evenings at the Hero of Waterloo getting plastered, then the nights tossing and turning, trying not to dream, and then many days sleeping in, trying to forget them. Yesterday he'd driven to Tamarama Beach for a bodysurf then lay on the hot sand to dry out, trying to clear his head as he peered at the topless girls through slit-eyes with his head resting on crossed arms, dreaming about Cassandra and Angela. The night before he hadn't gone to the pub but instead got a takeaway pizza and ate it in front of the television watching a new cartoon series called *The Simpsons*, then fell asleep on the lounge watching *Casablanca* on video.

He had only just reached his office when he got a page. He recognised the number as Casualty and Angela answered the phone. She'd heard from the secretaries that he was in and hoped he was all right since she hadn't heard from him. He said he'd been under the weather but was now feeling okay. She had a new admission in Casualty and he agreed to meet her there.

'Medical admin can't give us an intern so I've been holding the fort,' she said when they finally met.

Angela looked fresh and relaxed, as if it were she who had been on a break from work and not Walker. She seemed happy and bright.

'What about Sandy?' he asked.

'Gone back to Malaysia. His term was just about finished anyway. He wanted to see his parents.'

'And the police let him?'

'Looks like it.'

He didn't mention Gloria. 'Sorry you've had to do everything yourself. I'll speak to the clinical super today and see if we can get some help. Do we have many patients?'

'Twelve inpatients. Yesterday's clinic was quite large but I managed.'

He slapped his forehead. 'The clinic. I totally forgot. Angela, I'm so sorry.'

'You can't help being sick, Dr Walker.' She sounded sincere. He felt guilty. He noticed she didn't use his first name.

He scratched his chin, feeling uneasy. 'Did Aaron Young get home? The fellow who was fitting?'

Angela smiled. 'Yes, the scans were all clear. No cancer recurrence. He's started plasma exchange and is a lot better. His fits have stopped.'

'For the moment,' grumbled Walker.

She raised her hands. 'It's all we can do.'

They were in a short corridor where the linen trolleys were kept, away from the emergency room and the main thoroughfare. Walker felt as if she'd manoeuvred him to the quiet spot on purpose and he began to feel uneasy.

There were so many unanswered questions. Why did she have the metoprolol? Why did she keep the knowledge about what her father had done to her mother to herself? Did she really know nothing about her father's activities after the war?

Why had she slept with him?

He decided to ask a less contentious question. 'Are Barry and Cassandra still seeing each other?'

She rolled her eyes. 'Are they ever! I can't get rid of him. They spend most nights together, and they're so noisy!'

'Seems they really like each other then.'

'Well, they like each other's bodies at least.' She wrinkled her forehead. 'And I can confirm that he's still got a thing about the Phantom. He wears a ring when he comes over. I think he even has a costume. Dresses up for Cassie.' They both laughed. Then she became serious. 'But yes, I think they actually suit each other. They might even last.'

*And what about us?* was the unspoken question Walker did not want to ask.

'I think it was a mistake,' said Angela.

'What?' Is she talking about us?

She was looking directly at him, dark brown eyes beneath a flawless forehead. 'I think it was a mistake us sleeping together.'

'Ah, yes, I agree,' he said slowly. But he wasn't sure he *did* agree.

'I'm glad you agree.' She looked away. 'I don't like that side of myself. Those traits can run in families.'

Walker wasn't sure what she meant but before he could ask, she was looking at him again.

'We need to be able to work together, at least for the rest of this year, and that sort of thing will just complicate things immensely.'

'Sure, sure,' he said shortly, screwing up his mouth.

'You sound angry.'

'No, not at all.' He looked back into her eyes. 'But if we are going to work together, I think I deserve the truth.'

'What do you mean?'

'The metoprolol. Why did you have a bag of it and why did you throw it away?'

She was silent for some moments. Then she raised her head defiantly. 'I'll tell you that if you tell me the truth about your wife.'

'My wife?' Walker was bewildered. He'd spent the last three days trying *not* to think of his wife. 'What has that got to do with anything?'

She continued to stare at him silently. Then finally, 'We all have our secrets, Christopher. Are you ready to share yours?'

He looked away. No. No, I'm not ready. He would never be ready.

He turned to her. 'You said you had a new admission.'

Angela gave a subtle, knowing smile as she glanced down at her notes. 'Yes. A young fellow called Justin Davis. He's got chronic schizophrenia and has presented with a large mediastinal mass. And the other thing, he's been complaining of tender breasts for the last three months.'

'Tender breasts,' Walker said absently. 'Could be his medications. But I bet you he has a mediastinal germ cell tumour. The hormones released by the tumour are causing the breast enlargement ...' He took on a lecturing tone and began to walk towards the emergency room.

'Of course, Dr Walker,' said Angela, smiling confidently as she followed behind him. 'What else would it be ...'

### END OF BOOK 1

The story continues in
*Death in a Chapel*

## Author's note

THE MAIN CHARACTERS in this novel are completely fictional. If you think you recognise yourself or someone you have worked with, then you're wrong!

This might disappoint some who think this series is some sort of exposé of a Sydney teaching hospital. Of course, like any story, all characters and situations are necessarily based on memories of real people and events. But I can assure you that all main characters are the product of my imagination.

There are many historical names that are obviously real. I have never met any of these people and any mention of them in the book is a construction of events from public records.

Many of the historical details are accurate, such as contemporary news items, names of songs and television shows, and the names and position of restaurants and pubs in Sydney in 1991. Some details are inaccurate and I intentionally departed from the facts for the purposes of this fictional story. One such example is Darling House, a grand Georgian building in Lower Fort Street, The Rocks, which was not used as a nursing home in until 1994, three years after the setting of the book.

Some facts surrounding the assassination of the British high commissioner in Malaya have been distorted for the purposes of the story, although the names of those involved and most of the circumstances described are accurate.

The medical cases are descriptions of events I or my colleagues have been involved with over the years, although the patient names are fictional.

Discover other titles by Howard Gurney

Path to Chaos series (fantasy)
*Twin*
*The Thread Frays*
*Chaos*

Dr Christopher Walker Murder Mystery series
*Murder on the Ward*
*Death in a Chapel*
*Murder at The Rocks*


Thank you for reading my book. If you enjoyed it, please take a moment to leave a review at your favourite retailer.

Thanks!
Howard Gurney


www.howardgurney.com

@HowardGurney

Lightning Source UK Ltd.
Milton Keynes UK
UKHW040612200120
357267UK00001B/37

9 780648 717706